BLADE
USA TODAY BESTSELLING AUTHOR
MANDY HARBIN

To Aaron...because you love stabby things...and, thankfully, quirky writer chicks with a penchant for writing plans in pencil. Because sometimes, the only pointy tool you need in life is one that can erase the path you're on and give you means to jot down another.

*Okay, maybe **you** need more tools than that. And by need, I mean want. #knifelife.*

Regardless, not a day goes by that I'm not grateful our futures were rewritten.

May your blades always be sharp, Aaron, and your life never ever dull. Thank you for sharing it with me.

This book is for you.

CHAPTER ONE

He knew it was a dream.

Blade's sister had been dead fifteen years, but she stood there before him, the scent of lavender as much of a ghost as she was. He never understood why a seventeen-year-old girl wanted to smell like flowers, but Brenna surely did. Maybe it had been her fascination with the color purple that led to her floral obsession. She had always gravitated toward anything sporting shades of dark pink through magenta. He hadn't had a problem with that. He never did care for the smell, though.

And now it—those scents of lavender *and* blood—haunted his dreams, his sister's lifeless body standing there as she stared off into nothing, rather than resting on the gurney as he remembered seeing her when he came to identify her remains. This recurring dream used to freak him out, but now he knew when he'd wake up, he'd instantly miss the morbid sight. Not because he wanted to relive that day, rather he knew these fleeting moments were all he'd ever have of her again.

"Where's Jeremiah?"

He knew his sister was going to ask that, because she always did.

His answer never deviated. "In Hell."

"Was it you?" she asked as tears welled in her lifeless eyes. Blade was glad she didn't look at him. It would tear his heart out every time he dreamed about her.

"Yes," he said without emotion. That sonofabitch had killed his baby sister. Of course he'd hurt him. He'd made him bleed out of many holes.

Her scream was bloodcurdling, and Blade bolted upright in his bed before he awakened fully. He blinked into the darkness and groaned at the sudden throbbing headache as the dream's intensity subsided.

"Damn tequila," he muttered as he tossed the sheets off him. Oh, he couldn't blame the dream on the alcohol, but the pickaxe pounding into his skull he could. He rubbed his face as he stood, knowing it wouldn't help his state any, but doing it regardless. Drowning his sorrows in liquor wasn't the answer, but it sure dulled the pain.

Not that he was still hurting over the loss of his sister. He loved her, sure, and missed her terribly but that was fifteen years ago. Even when he dreamed about her, he no longer felt that all-consuming, crushing pain. Time had scabbed over those wounds. No, the new ache he'd been self-medicating with a bottle of Jose Cuervo was all because of one little FBI agent.

Anna Sue Fisher.

Jesus, the woman gutted him, and the worst part was he didn't even know why. He hadn't known her very long. Only worked with her briefly once before they'd been assigned to the Oberman case. Something changed in him when he'd been working with her, and spending a couple of months in close quarters had been too much for his growing attraction. One night, he'd given into his desire, and she'd been so hot and passionate for him that something within him had snapped. Never in his life had he ever wanted to just *be* with a woman before.

As in have her and not let her go.

He'd been happy hopping from one bed to another, playing the field. He treated women with the utmost respect, but he'd never been one to settle down. That night, though, with her in his arms, he'd felt this overwhelming need to possess her in every sense.

Anna, on the other hand, had other plans. The morning after their night of passion, she'd thrown up walls and wouldn't speak of what had happened between them. Before he knew it, he was back in Arkansas, and she'd flown off to wherever the feds stationed her. It wasn't as if the bureau needed her in this town after his best friend and fellow Bang Shift crew member, Brody "Brutus" Jackson, killed Xan's sinister mafia boss ex-husband. Working with the FBI, it had been their assignment to protect that woman, but even back then he'd felt there was something a little special about Anna. They'd lost touch after that assignment, but working together again had ignited whatever he'd felt for her before into raw, carnal desire.

Then Anna had left, and Blade hadn't heard from her since.

Not one word.

Normally, he wouldn't have cared. It was easier when the woman of the day—or afternoon—walked away first. Anna was different, though. He knew it, just didn't know why.

And she was gone.

His heart seized as he grabbed his pants, foregoing a shower. No, she wasn't *gone* like his sister. Just out of his life, and that was the bitch of it. There was a time he would have denied himself a woman like her because he hadn't been worthy.

Hell, maybe he would never be.

Images of Brenna flitted through his mind as he dressed. He grabbed the cheap body spray to douse some of the tequila seeping through his pores. He'd just get dirty again and shower tonight when he got home from the shop like he did last night and every evening after working his shift. A quick squirt of hair gel, and an overly long tooth brushing, and he was as ready as he was going to be.

Before grabbing his shop and motorcycle keys, he reached into his nightstand and pulled out his combat knife, so old the engraving had long worn off. He studied the cold steel he carried every day along with a second pocket knife and remembered again the last time he'd used it.

The day he'd killed Jeremiah Ward.

He turned to leave, but stopped midway when he caught his reflection in the bathroom mirror. He stared at his hair, unblinking, knife still in his grip. The guys of the Bang Shift crew gave him hell over his spiked 'do, thinking his handle had come naturally from his choice of hairstyles.

He glanced down at the blade in his hand, even though he hadn't needed a reminder that the name had nothing do to with any spikes on his head. He'd just never corrected their assumption.

It was easier that way. Much, much easier. He liked when his skeletons stayed buried. Except for when he slept, he had no problem shoving them away and pretending things were normal. It was under the cloak of darkness when they pushed their way to the surface that he had no way of ignoring them. But in all honesty, there was no getting away from his past.

Didn't stop him from trying to be Mr. Happy-Go-Lucky, cracking jokes and flirting with just about every woman who crossed his path. He'd been fortunate enough that embracing life that way helped him ignore the painful reminder of his youth. But he'd had a hell of a time keeping a smile on his face ever since Anna Sue blew into his life and left on the same breeze. He had a new ache now, one that wrenched those old feelings shortly after Brenna died front and center.

He might not feel that crushing pain regularly anymore over *that* horrible loss, but he coped the same way. Looking for answers to all his life's questions at the bottom of tequila bottles. Damn answers he needed were never there.

But these feelings now made one thing crystal clear... he'd never be worthy of any woman. Because no matter what he did or how often he put on a happy face going about his regular routine, deep down he knew there was no escaping who he really was.

Blade Young was a killer.

A stone-cold, ruthless murderer.

Not worthy of Anna Sue Fisher?

Fuck, but there really was no doubt about it.

———

ANNA SUE SCROLLED through their case list on her tablet as she awaited her supervisor to show. There wasn't enough coffee on the planet for these early Monday meetings, and not because they were usually first thing in the morning. Rick McMillan, their shrewd team leader, usually spent a good portion going over policies and government red tape with the agents on the team. Time Anna would rather spend chasing leads and arresting the bad guys. Sitting still for a couple of hours in the morning when her defenses weren't up yet gave her too much of an opportunity to get lost in her thoughts, and that was something she couldn't handle. Ever since the Oberman case six months ago, she'd kept her nose in a file and her soles pounding the pavement as if the devil himself was on her heels. Focusing on other people breaking the law distracted her from her own bad decisions.

Well, *one* bad decision.

One tall, lean, muscled, spiky-blond-hair bad decision.

Braxton "Blade" Young.

Damn, but if that man wasn't sex personified, and he sure as hell knew it. He was a walking god, the type of man who'd make the surliest of women giggle in delight when he aimed that thousand-watt smile of his at them. He had his pick of any number of women, and Anna was sure none he'd set his sights on had been able to resist him. Blade flirting was a charmer, but Blade on a mission to have a woman moaning beneath him was a powerhouse of lethal lust. Anna was certain the man never failed to get what he wanted.

And she should know. He'd conquered her.

Oh, she'd giggled at his harmless flirting when they'd worked on that case together in Dallas. He'd quickly become the star of her masturbatory fantasies—a fact she'd felt slightly guilty about. She'd never thought of any colleague that way, and she'd never *ever* dated anybody she worked with. No way was she going to shit where she ate. But, technically, Blade wasn't an FBI agent, so she'd allowed herself those few images of him in the darkest of nights. A little something to take the edge off of working so close with him, she'd told herself. But as the time passed, his easygoing nudges and winks and smiles turned into something heated and forbidden. He'd made her a million promises in those half-mast gazes, making her forget all the reasons why sleeping with him would be a bad idea.

It had been a terrible idea.

He'd delivered on every one of those sinful promises.

Thinking back to that night, she still couldn't remember when they'd gone past the point of no return. From suggestion to full-on seduction. Before she knew it, she'd been on her knees before him, worshiping his cock and getting drunk on his very essence.

And that right there threw her. She'd spent the days and weeks following berating herself for giving in to the temptation that was Blade. Yes, the guy was hot, but when it came down to it, Anna had never had a problem wrangling her libido. She was pretty good at not only dishing out the rejections, but downright ignoring any man who came onto her.

Not that she drew the attention of the opposite sex often. Oh, no. She was pretty homely compared to most women. And when it came to her female colleagues in this room, Shelby Landry and Viola Lane, there was zero comparison. Those girls could double as models. Hell, they were both currently working undercover at a massage clinic, rubbing backs and arresting asses.

Anna had accepted a long time ago she was average in the looks department. She'd grown up in the Midwest where beans and cornbread were staples and perfecting fried chicken was a rite-of-passage. She was fit, of course, because she had to be able to chase down suspects. Although, she'd taken a hiatus from jogging after breaking her ankle six months ago. It had been slow going getting back into her regular routine. No matter how much she exercised, her thighs never sported a gap, and no matter how much she'd prayed growing up, her boobs never advanced to a C cup. She didn't wear makeup expertly like Viola and didn't have that natural beauty thing going on like Shelby. She was just plain ol' Anna Sue Fisher from a corn farm in Kansas.

She didn't know if Blade had seen her as just another conquest or if he'd been truly attracted to her. Even if his plans were of the hit-it-and-quit-it variety, he was a complete gentleman. Outside of the bedroom, he wasn't a kiss-and-tell man, and for that she was so, so grateful.

How could she face her boss and teammates if they knew what happened back in Dallas? She was too smart to claim his attentiveness threw her off her game, yet she didn't understand logically how he'd been able to seduce her. Was it still called seduction if the woman practically begged for it? Not only had she been unable to muster the strength to push him away, she distinctly remembered grabbing his shirt and pulling him even closer to her the night he'd rocked her world. Jesus, it was as if she couldn't drop to her knees fast enough.

He'd been *sooo*—

"Are you doing some online shopping?" Shelby asked, yanking Anna from her thoughts of Blade and that naughty night.

She blinked a few times before looking over to the youngest agent in their group. Darrell, one of the men on the team, had taken Shelby under his wing and shown her the ropes. She'd caught on quickly and would be ready to work a case solo in no time. "No. Researching leads on our pending cases." Technically not accurate, but that was what she'd had open on her tablet. No need to tell her teammate how distracting one night with one man was six months ago.

"Jeez, you're such a workhorse," Viola said from across the table.

"You could learn a thing or two from her," Carson said.

Darrell Tobin and Carson Childers were the two men on the small special team Rick put together a couple of years ago. They usually focused on financial crimes. They each had their specialties. Anna was a forensic accountant, and since "crime pays" was the outlaws' motto, she had her hand in just about every case that came their way. She was good at chasing the money.

"Screw you," Viola said with a toss of her blonde hair.

"Your husband wouldn't be too happy if you did that." Carson winked at her.

Viola opened her mouth, but snapped it shut when the door opened.

"Morning," Darrell said as he walked in and took his seat. He looked as if he just rolled out of bed.

"You okay?" Shelby asked.

He chuckled. "Yeah. Long night going over some international docs. I'm going to need your linguistic expertise, I think."

"No problem. We can meet up afterward."

Rick walked in then and sat at the head of the table. "Good morning, everyone. We've got a lot to discuss, so let's skip over the morning pleasantries and start with last week's updates."

Anna listened dutifully as her boss discussed events of meetings that occurred above her pay grade. Nothing really new. Budget-cuts-this, need-to-work-with-other-agencies-that. Crisis averted over here. Problems with intel other there. Blah, blah, blah. She didn't understand why he felt the need to share every detail about politics when nothing was really different, and most everything had come across in various emails anyway. After what felt like an eternity, he took a deep breath.

"Any questions before we move on?" he finally asked.

She glanced around the room and noticed the same bored expressions on her teammates' faces. At least she wasn't the only one who didn't care about that part of the meeting.

"Next up, assignments. Viola, Shelby, how's the massage therapy case coming?"

"ICE has a lead on a trafficker," Shelby said. Anna couldn't stop the small smile that formed at the newbie's drive. "Should make an arrest in a day or two."

"And my hands have never been this soft," Viola said.

Rick gave a quick shake of his head and said, "Always looking at the bright side."

"Yes, sir."

"ICE still has point on the case. We'll continue assisting if their suspect fizzles out, but I'm putting you two on other assignments as of today. Lane, you're working with Childers on the Princesses Robbers case."

"Two bored, privileged socialites suspected of a series of bank heists. Got it," Carson said, then added, "Don't know why they didn't just start a YouTube channel."

"YouTube is dead. It's all Insta now," Shelby said.

"We don't know for sure it's the Wellingtons," Viola said glancing between them.

"Agreed," Rick added, effectively stopping any more discussion on that. "Landry, I'm putting you on assignment with Fisher," he said, first looking at Shelby before focusing on Anna Sue. "I need you on location for this."

She tossed up a silent *thank you*, eager for the in-depth distraction. She couldn't even sit in a meeting room for five minutes before her brain drifted against her mental Blade boundaries. Getting away, throwing herself into work, was just what she needed. Distance and the right kind of distraction.

"You two are flying into Little Rock this afternoon."

What the—*Oh no.* No, no, no.

The look on her face must have been telling because Rick's gaze narrowed. "You have a problem with Arkansas?"

Yes. Well, not the state, just one particular inhabitant. The further she could stay away from Blade, the better. And now her boss wanted her to work a case near him? That was too much for her body to handle. She liked being a state away from Blade and his hold on her. But it wasn't as if she could tell Rick any of this or even be vague about not liking Arkansas. This was her job. She swallowed, pushing down her panic along with the sudden lump in her throat. This would be fine. Blade didn't live in the city. Hell, he didn't even live in the same county. Maybe it wouldn't be so bad. Who said she would even have to cross the river? It could be her new geographical boundary. "No, sir," she answered automatically, hoping the moment between his question and her answer hadn't dragged by as it had felt to her.

"Good." He looked down and opened a file. "I need you to meet up with the Bang Shift crew."

Fuuuuuuuck. Her eyes closed, her silent thanks from before morphing into a string of colorful curse words. This could not be happening! She wasn't just going to be in the same state, or even the same town. Anna was going to have to work with Blade.

Again.

Shit. Triple fucking shit, shitty shit!

"Fisher," Rick said tersely.

Looking up quickly, she said, "Sorry, sir."

"What's your problem?"

I boinked Blade while on assignment, and ran from him like an awkward chicken. Please, don't make me face him. She didn't think that response would fly, so she improvised. "Arkansas is miserable in the summer," she said, hoping to make light of it. No matter what, she would try to maintain her professionalism while in front of her superior. She'd embrace her bad-assery FBI agent persona right now. Later, she could be all girly about this and drown her sorrows the best way she knew how. With her trusty friends Ben and Jerry.

He flashed a half smile. "It does get humid there." Then his face grew serious. "You could be there a while, so pack accordingly."

Great.

"I thought we sent them assignments, not agents," Darrell said, and she was relieved to have the group's attention focused on him now. "Well, except for Gauge."

Anna had turned to Darrell, but at the mention of Gauge, she couldn't help notice Viola stiffen. Word around the office was she and Gauge had a thing when they were at Quantico, but nothing had been confirmed by either. Anna figured it was why the lady across from her had never been the one to go to Arkansas when dealing with the Bang Shift...even if Viola was now happily married to another man.

"Gauge is one of them. His allegiance is with those men."

"He's still an agent," Viola quickly said before adding, "And *those men* are still government contractors."

"They're hired guns. Never forget they'd kill for the highest bidder," Rick said.

"I don't think that's a fair assessment, sir," Anna said, taken aback by her boss's words. "I've been down there several times and never got that vibe from them. Gruff? Sure. And tough as nails, but not gun-toting extremists."

"They're mercenaries," Darrell said with exasperation. "Colonel brought those guys together, and he was an evil bastard. They sure as hell ain't a bunch of Boy Scouts."

"Just because Gauge's life is the only one not a mystery to us, doesn't mean he can't be influenced by his family."

"His brother's in the military," Shelby said, frowning. "So is mine. We've both talked about their tours. Most people consider that a *noble* profession."

"There's a lot you don't know," Rick said. "And not all family is blood."

Anna frowned, not liking how this conversation was going. Yes, Colonel had been the leader of the crew in Mayflower, Arkansas, until they'd learned he was in cahoots with the mob, a life-threatening reality for everyone, especially Brody and Xan. But the feds trusted them enough to work with them. They went to those guys for assignments. Maybe Rick's attitude now was politically charged, like the budget cuts he'd discussed earlier. It wasn't as if the work the Bang Shift crew did for the government was out of the goodness of their hearts. Maybe she should've paid more attention to that part of the meeting.

Whatever the reason for his personal feelings on the working relationship, it didn't change the fact that there was some new threat that necessitated her going back to the state she never wanted to set foot in again. Several possible scenarios flitted through her mind. Most obvious being that there could be a new threat of Brody's old mafia connections showing up, guns blazing. But if it involved Brody—or Xan through Marco's family—Jack Parsons's RICO team would handle the case. Anna Sue had been on assignment in Arkansas when Jack needed extra eyes on Brody and his buddies because she'd already been familiar with the inner workings of the crime family's financial and illegal activity. But Jack's team spearheaded that. Unless the Bang Shift needed one of them to assist, as was the case with Hunter's sister, or other cases involving national security took precedence, her team focused on the financial aspects of various crimes.

"And that's why the SEC wants us to have a closer look."

"The SEC?" Carson asked, leaning back.

"Closer look at what?" Anna asked at the same time, gaze narrowing at Rick. She couldn't explain why the hairs on the back of her neck suddenly stood. If the SEC was involved then it made sense why her team was being pulled in. But that just raised a bunch more questions as to how the Bang Shift came into play in all of this.

"Not sure I like your attitude, Fisher."

She took a silent breath. "Those guys aren't white-collar. I'm trying to understand what the SEC wants with them."

He focused on the other members of the team and answered, "They're investigating an investment firm and want us to look into a new executive. Mason Showalter. I'm pulling intel on him, but as of right now, this isn't one of our typical forensic accounting cases." His gaze slid back to Anna. "Mr. Showalter has a connection to one of the Bang Shift crew members."

Who? Though the cold dread flowing through her answered that silent question.

"Braxton Young, a.k.a. Blade, receives a call from him on the twenty-fifth of every month. I want to know why. We don't know enough about that group of guys in Mayflower. I'm meeting with Jack Parsons...again...to talk about them.

Frankly, I feel we need to determine if continued working relations with the Bang Shift and *any* FBI team is the way to go."

"But the federal government has been relying on them for years to handle contracts," Viola said.

"Even though we've learned Colonel made no bones about sealing records and obliterating their pasts and most family connections, we still continue to work with them. Put the lives of citizens in their hands. Two of those men had mafia connections to two different crime families. Now this? We should be able to identify the connection of Mason Showalter and Braxton Young with a few clicks on a keyboard. We can't. Colonel had been methodical, so we really have no idea who these men are. Who the hell knows what else we'll find. This is exactly why anytime someone tried hiring an external group to handle government business, I have always been against it."

Anna's heart thudded in her chest, her emotions pinging all over as a memory came drifting back. One particularly long, boring night of surveillance, Blade had told her something about himself, and it had totally caught her off guard.

"Blade was arrested once," she heard herself say.

Rick's eyes narrowed. "When?"

"I, um, I don't know. He told me when we were watching Heather Anderson. Didn't volunteer any details, though." She'd later tried to look up specifics of his crime, but found nothing. She'd figured it was something minor. Maybe public intox with short probation and a guaranteed clean record at the end if he stayed out of trouble. Something small that wouldn't leave a record. She'd dismissed the small confession almost as quickly as he'd made it. But maybe it was something bigger than the average misdemeanor. Colonel had definitely been meticulous enough to want everything on his men locked tight or completely erased from the system. Not that it would've been necessary if they were just mercenaries. That particular job didn't require a clean record to take hits. But to work with the federal government? Now, that was a different story.

"Well, now. The fact he felt free enough to confide in you makes you the perfect choice to go. Love it when my instincts are right."

Oh, the bad feeling she had grew stronger.

"So what's the cover?" Darrell asked. "Because we can't tell the men she's there to pry into Blade's life."

Pry? Anna was gonna be sick. Her emotions were all over. On the one hand, they trusted those men and now she was being tasked with going behind their backs...one back in particular. On the other hand, she really had no idea what Blade had done in his past. Or what was he doing now. When it all came down to it, she didn't really know him at all. Not that *that* changed how she felt about him. Or the fact that those guys had worked with the government for years, taking many of the shit jobs they either didn't want to do or couldn't because of red tape. They'd skirted the law for the sake of justice, and now they could be punished for the very thing the government paid them to do.

This had disaster written all over it.

"There's a hunting lodge in Louisiana he goes to every year. Two years ago, he bought some shares in the business. A developer's buying surrounding land. We're going in under the guise of investigating the developer."

"Those guys know we primarily focus on the money, but if we tell them we're working with the SEC, they'd have questions as to why that branch is involved," Viola said.

"Agreed," Rick said. "Instead of telling them we've partnered with the SEC, we'll say we're working with the IRS. That agency gets everyone's attention. Since Blade is linked to the business, it should make him want to help and be an easy *in* with him." Rick looked at Anna. "Though it seems you already have one."

She kept her mouth shut and hoped her face didn't give anything away.

"And we just expect the Bang Shift to help investigate this bogus developer in hopes of finding the connection of Mason Showalter to Blade Young without offering a contract for their services?" Carson laughed without humor. "Guns *for hire* don't work for free."

"Unless it's personal," Anna added, remembering the call about Flint Willis and the massive drug bust.

"It wouldn't have been personal if Mr. Knight had reported Mr. Willis as soon as he was propositioned." Even though Anna knew Bear's last night, it was weird hearing him called anything other than his nickname. "They screwed the pooch on that, too. We still haven't been able to locate Flint Willis."

"We've seen some card activity out west," Carson said. "We'll find him."

"Good. Anyway, we'll give the Bang Shift the you-scratch-my-back-I'll-scratch-yours spiel." Rick shrugged. "There are budget cuts, and they need us if they want to keep getting money."

"Assuming we don't find reason to and stop contracting with them anyway," Viola said. Anna could hear the discomfort in her voice and was glad she wasn't the only one who seemed to have a problem with this assignment. And she wasn't even thinking of the big, fat personal reason.

"Nothing is ever guaranteed," Rick said.

"So Anna gets close to Blade for the SEC's inquiry into Showalter. And Shelby's role?" Darrell asked.

Rick looked to Shelby. "I want you at the shop, watching, seeing if you can learn anything else about the other men. To them, you're a peace offering sent to help with *legal* contracts and work at the shop since they'll be a man short. You remember basic auto repair?"

Shelby smiled. "Yes, sir. Grew up running around my daddy's garage in Nebraska. When other little girls were playing with Barbie, I was learning how to rebuild a carburetor."

Carson chuckled. "Can't see you as a grease monkey."

Shelby winked. "I'm really good at lubing a chassis."

Darrell growled. "Not funny."

Rick's lip twitched, but that was the only sign of humor he showed. "Good. Fit in with the guys, and see what you can learn." He's gaze cut to Anna. "We need to learn everything we can about these men. Starting with Young. No matter what, you stick to him like glue. Find out about this Showalter man and report back. But, Fisher, solving that is just scratching the surface. By the end of this mission, I want you to know more about Braxton Young than he knows himself. Understood?"

With confidence she didn't feel, Anna gave him a quick nod. "Understood."

How could she get close to him without letting her defenses down? It would be a miracle if she could do her job without getting too emotionally close to Blade. She avoided him after their night together for a reason, but that didn't mean she stopped thinking about him, hoping at her weaker moments that maybe he could be different, that there could be more with him.

None of that mattered now. None of it.

This assignment would forever shatter even the tiniest of dreams where she and Blade had a future. Because even if they considered picking up where they'd left off after that night of passion, she'd never be able to tell him why she was *really* coming back six months later.

And if he ever learned the truth, Blade would never forgive her.

CHAPTER TWO

"Glad you decided to join us today, brother," Brody said, looking from under a '64 Corvette's hood as Blade walked into the Bang Shift Garage. It was where the guys of the crew worked as mechanics by day and mercenaries by night. The feds had dubbed their team *the bang shift* because they were the pseudo third shift working alongside the FBI, not that the feds were their only client, but where the feds were concerned, the group was an off the books team who took some government contracts when the powers that be wanted to avoid that troublesome red tape. The guys either spent their time banging gears or shooting—*banging*—their guns, so the moniker fit. Once Colonel was taken out, Bear became their fearless leader and renamed the garage to the team's name. No one outside their group would get the true meaning, apart from the FBI agents they worked with, and there weren't many. Blade considered them a necessary evil and usually avoided any interactions with them. Except for Gauge who was a permanent fixture of the crew.

And Anna Sue who was a constant figure on his mind.

"Yeah, yeah," Blade grumbled as he passed Brody, but

gave him a light shoulder check and a smirk as he walked by to get in his grease-stained jumper.

"Damn, did ya bathe in Beam?" Brody said.

"Jim and I are on a first name basis."

"Smells like he's your bitch."

Blade suppressed a wince. He'd been hungover every day this week. A trend he started oh, about six months ago. Some days he hadn't shown up quite this bad, but that just meant he'd been too tired the night before to get *too* shit faced. Brody was like a brother to him, and the man had said something to him about his drinking on more than one occasion. Usually, he pulled him aside away from judging eyes. The fact that his closest friend blurted it out right in the middle of the garage was proof that the whiskey Blade drank last night was trying to escape out of his pores.

Blade wadded up his jumper. "I'll take a quick shower." Not that he figured it'd help, but it couldn't hurt.

"You got twenty minutes," Bear called out. "Team meeting at eight."

Blade didn't even look over his shoulder to see who all stood around. He knew everybody had already arrived at the shop by the vehicles in the parking lot, so it was possible every member of their team had been in earshot of the reprimand. He silently cussed as he made his way to the bathroom off the shop. It wasn't large, but working on cars got messy. The shower came in handy for when one of the guys needed to freshen up before heading somewhere.

Or when one of them had more alcohol in their system than blood.

After shucking his clothes, he showered, using the heavy degreaser, stripping all the natural oils, and hopefully stale booze, from his body. He washed three times. Once he finished, he dug out his bag of essentials stored in the cabinet and brushed his teeth the same number of times he washed his balls, gargled, and dressed. He sprayed some cologne on, too, just to be on the safe side, before snapping into his coveralls.

When he walked out into the hall, he stumbled to a stop before running into Brody who leaned against the wall, arms crossed, watching as Blade exited.

"Sorry I said that out there, man. Wasn't cool to rag you like that."

He shifted his weight, unable to hide his uneasiness. "It's all right. I mean, I need a swift kick in the ass."

"Yeah, you do." Brody sighed. "But I should've pulled you outside rather than ream you in the bays."

"Don't worry about it." Blade began to walk around him.

Brody stuck his arm out to stop him. "I worry about you."

Blade's gaze cut to his closest buddy. "I know." What else could he say? He knew he was in complete self-destruct mode. But he couldn't seem to find a good reason to get off this runaway train to Hell.

"Why don't you come over to dinner tonight? Xan put on a pot roast this morning."

"Sure, yeah, sounds good." The thought of hanging around Brody's domestic bliss had him craving another Beam and cola, though he wouldn't dare admit that. Brody was happy for the first time in his life, and no matter how shitty Blade's life was right now, he didn't want to rain on the guy's parade.

"Xan's pregnant."

Blade gaped at Brody. Did he just hear him right? "What?" He stepped closer, his own problems momentarily forgotten. His long-time friend looked shell-shocked with a hint of panic laced in for good measure.

"Yeah. She took a pregnancy test yesterday. Going to the doctor this afternoon." Brody rubbed his head. "Gotta love small towns. She said when she was pregnant with Scott it took a week to get in to see a doctor, and he'd been on Marco's payroll." Brody scowled. It was obvious the man hated Xan's ex, and if he could kill him all over again, Blade was sure Brody would do it slowly to exact as much pain as possible each and every time.

"She seeing a doc in Conway or driving into Little Rock?"

"Conway. Her OBG-whatever's office is there. He delivers babies, too, so she won't have to find a new doc. Said Dr. Peters would give her all the time off she needed." He shoved his hands into his pockets and rocked on his heels. "Her nursing training kicked in the moment she found out about the baby. Shit. I'm gonna have a baby," he said in wonder, and Blade wasn't sure if the man had actually said that last sentence to Blade. It seemed as if Brody was lost in verbal thought.

"You're already a father to Scott," Blade said, trying to ease the man's fear. When that got no response, he added, "And you're practically my daddy, too." He smiled, waiting.

Oh yeah, that got Brody's attention. He glared at Blade and muttered, "Asshole. I'm not that much older than you."

Another thought occurred to him. "So, what's this mean for the wedding plans?" The two lovebirds were already in the process of making their relationship official.

Brody's gaze narrowed. "She wants to move it up."

"Whoa, whoa...I thought you wanted to run down the aisle ASAP. Why the pissed-off glare?"

"'Cause she refuses to cancel it and go to the courthouse. She wants the whole thing moved up. Like she wants the whole thing still, but much sooner. Roc's gonna chap my ass when I ask him if we can do it sometime within the next few weeks. He gave me hell for asking to use his barn for the wedding—"

"He told Xan she was more than welcome to have it at his place," Blade said, cutting off Brody's grumble. "He just ragged you because it was an opportunity to let his asshole side shine through."

"Because he keeps it under lock and key all the time," Brody said sarcastically, and Blade couldn't blame him. Roc was the meanest son of bitch on the team. "Besides that hard ass, we have to see if the caterer, florist, baker, photographer, DJ ,and God knows who else can all accommodate the change, which isn't likely, and we have to notify all the guests of the new date because the *Save the Date* notices went out several months ago. Then the invitations went out about six weeks ago. Money wasted, deposits probably blown, plus more money for priority scheduling and rush orders. Jesus, I just want to sign the papers and be done with it."

Blade clapped him on the back and nudged him to start walking toward the meeting room, so they wouldn't be late. "I know, man. But you remember how many stores she went to looking for the perfect dress, and when she finally found it how excited she was? Dude, that woman acted like she'd just inherited a 1969 Camaro ZL1."

Brody barked out a laugh. "Now that'd be something to get excited about."

"Damn, I get a hard-on just thinking about driving one of those."

"No shit."

They walked into the room and leaned against the table

on the right-side wall. "Can't blame the woman for wanting to fit into the dress of her dreams," Blade said gently, hoping Brody hadn't complained to his soon-to-be-wife about the sudden change in nuptials.

"Yeah, and she's freaking out about the pregnancy. She thinks she's hiding it, but I know her."

"She's not the only one freaking out." Blade cut his gaze to Brody.

"A baby," he said in wonder. "I mean, yeah, Scott is mine, but he was a teenager when I came along...the second time." Brody half-smiled. "There wasn't any midnight feedings and pre-dawn diaper changes."

"And how cool is it that you get to experience that with Xan?"

"Yeah." Brody smiled, and for the first time since walking in, he finally seemed to relax a little. But then his focus zeroed in on Blade. "But I need you to deal with whatever shit has you drinking your life away. I need to know if something ever happens to me you got my back. I ain't got any family. *You're* my brother."

"Hell, Brody." Blade tried not to blush, but felt his cheeks warm. "I love you, too, man."

"So you'll break up with Jim?"

Blade sighed. "He's lousy in bed anyway."

Brody chuckled. "True that."

Hunter walked into the room, followed by Gauge and Roc. Gauge and Hunter leaned against the table opposite Blade and Brody. Roc hopped up on the table beside Blade. Roc wasn't one to buddy up with anyone in particular, but the man was smart enough to steer clear of Hunter.

And still Hunter stared daggers at Roc from across the small room.

When Hunter's sister, Heather, returned to

Mayflower earlier in the year, after she and her friend, Maya, had gotten caught up in some trouble, Roc had taken a sudden interest in Heather. Over the last several months, that interest had only intensified, which led to even more trash-talk between the two men at the garage. Blade had been too wrapped up in his own crap to know what was going on between Roc and Heather...if anything really was. But whatever was going down had Hunter in full big-brother mode. Of course, Roc was the type of man to goad the other just because. Blade wouldn't be surprised if nothing was going on between Roc and Heather, and the sadistic shithead was enjoying pissing off his fellow teammate.

"Sorry, I'm running a few minutes behind," Bear said as he walked in and sat on the edge of the table facing the others. Blade wondered why they even had chairs in this meeting room. The guys never used them. "Been on the phone with the feds."

Blade stiffened. There hadn't been much communication with the feds since the op in Dallas involving Hunter's sister. It'd all come to a head outside Conway. Heather—and Xan, Roxie, and Maya for that matter—had been rescued, and Anna had been shipped to her next FBI assignment, wherever that was. If something could be successful and also a clusterfuck, it'd describe that. Lots of salt had been poured into wounds.

Since then, the guys had taken a few private gigs in what had become an impromptu downtime, but for the most part, they'd been playing catch-up at the shop. The call and the sudden meeting meant only one thing. There was a new federal case that needed their attention.

Assignments were what they lived for. It was the reason they were brought together in the first place. Granted,

Colonel had been the driving force behind that, but he was long gone. The guys were finding their own way now.

Some of these assignments were shadier than others... and that included ones the government tossed their way. The more unsavory, the bigger the paycheck. With how Blade was dragging through life right now, he needed the distraction more than the dollar bills. This couldn't have come at a better time.

Bear looked at him, but didn't say anything. Blade stared back, eagerly waiting.

"I need you sober for this. Or you're on the bench."

Fuck. He should've known that was coming.

"Already told Brody I'm capping the bottle."

More silence.

"I'll make sure he sticks with it," Brody said.

"He's not going to have you around to check, but I'm sure the feds will keep me updated on it."

"Does that mean—"

"Yes," Bear said, cutting Blade off. "They asked for you specifically." The question *why* was on the tip of his tongue, but before he could get it out, Bear continued. "They're sending a couple of agents out here. You'll assist one with gathering intel for a case they're working on. The other has garage experience and will help at the shop since you'll be busy on the case. She'll also assist the primary as needed."

"She?" Hunter asked.

Oh shit. Could they send Anna Sue to work in the shop? He had no idea if the woman knew anything about cars. But if she was coming, he didn't want her working at the shop while he was away working on some case. He wanted to work with her.

And that went completely against his resolve earlier that he wasn't good enough for her. Damn, he could be all noble with her when she was nowhere around, but put that beautiful woman in his line of sight and all reason fled.

He glanced around the room. His buddies had varying degrees of interest showing on their faces at the idea of a woman fixing up cars. At least that *better* be the source of their interest. He knew for at least two of them—Brody and Hunter—there was no sexual interest going on, but he couldn't be sure when it came to the other men.

"Yes, Agent Shelby Landry. Numbers geek. Father had a garage for forty years before retiring. She worked there while in high school and college."

Relief that Anna wouldn't be the one working in the garage came swiftly, followed by frustration. If she was the one being sent, he could've gotten her alone at some point to talk to her. Now that possibility was gone. *It's for the best.* He needed to remember that. Working near Anna Sue would be too much temptation for him to do the right thing where she was concerned, and that was leave her the hell alone. Even if he was an upstanding guy with an impeccable past, the woman still avoided him. Didn't matter if he couldn't go a day without thinking about her, the lady didn't want him. He'd do well to remember that.

"Never heard of her," Gauge said, frowning. He'd been an undercover FBI agent working with the team for years, still technically worked for them, but now his status was known to the rest of the team.

"She's a recent grad, but I'm told she works with someone you trained with. Viola Lane. Remember her?"

Gauge's eyes grew infinitesimally, but that was the only sign of recognition the hardened agent showed. "I do. Linguists expert. Works financial crimes for Rick McMillian."

Blade's gaze whipped to Gauge. Shelby and Viola

weren't names he recognized, but Rick McMillian rang a very big bell.

"Anna's supervisor," Blade breathed. Someone came into the garage, although the door's ding barely registered to Blade. He refused to look away, much less get up and interact with a customer. One minute he was relieved the object of his fantasies wasn't coming to tempt him, and the next he was back to damn near selling his soul to make it a reality.

Through the corner of his eye, he saw Hunter step out to assist whoever walked in.

"Correct," Bear said. "Rick sent Anna and Shelby. I've already stated what Shelby's role will be. You're working with Anna on her case."

Bear kept talking, but the words didn't break through the sudden fog of Blade's brain. Anna Sue was coming here. He wouldn't have to worry about trying to steal her away for a few moments to talk. He'd be working with her.

Again.

Memories of the last assignment they shared assailed him. They'd had hours alone together. Hours.

And it still hadn't been enough.

He could—

"Blade. I'm talking to you," Bear said.

Blade blinked at him. "Sorry." *Shit.* Daydreaming on the job was a rookie mistake. He needed to fucking focus.

"As I was saying, she's investigating a Louisiana development company. We haven't been hired to do a job. This is more of a combining-resources assignment."

"Translation, we're working for free," Roc said, scowling.

Bear sighed. "Rick said with the president's decision to sack the FBI director, the assistant director has had to step in. He's a dick, and he's scrutinizing everything. After what happened with Colonel, the new powers that be may decide to create an internal task force to handle what would normally be shuttled over to us. That means no more blank checks from Uncle Sam."

"Parsons wouldn't allow that to happen," Gauge said, crossing his arms.

"Jack Parsons isn't powerful enough to sway the bureau's decision, especially since it's currently in the political hot seat. But if the other teams we've worked alongside back him up, then yeah, we should be good."

"But if not?" Brody asked.

"If not and our relationship is severed," Bear looked at Gauge, "your ass could then be on the first flight back to the Dallas field office."

"And Xan could be thrown back into WINSEC," Brody growled.

"Yep," Bear said. "Which you'd follow her into witness protection, and we'd be down two men. Even if we continued taking jobs from the private sector, we wouldn't have enough resources in the field."

"Or in the garage," Roc said.

"So we'll play nice with the feds—"

"This *one* damn time," Roc said through gritted teeth, cutting Bear off.

"This one damn time," Bear agreed as Hunter walked back in. Blade's gaze landed on Hunter before focusing on Bear again. Then it shot back to the door. Hunter wasn't alone.

One woman who followed him in had long brown hair. Blade didn't recognize the lady, nor did his gaze stay on her. It was the other woman who held his attention.

Who caused his heart to pound in his ears, blood to rush in his veins...and then run south to his groin.

Anna.

She somehow was even more beautiful than he remembered, even though he'd catalogued every inch of her before. At this moment, he didn't care why she was here, what her objective was. Nor did he care about his earlier resolve.

Hell, he didn't even give a rat's ass about the specifics of this case. None of that was important.

All he cared about was, before Anna Sue Fisher left, he was going to get reacquainted with every part of her. Did she still smell like roses? God, he loved that about her.

And still he knew in the back of his mind, she was only here temporarily.

Blade knew deep down he'd have to find the strength to let her go all over again, and he'd be right back in the pit of all that pain. Probably much deeper than before.

She tucked her hair behind her ear, and he remembered just how sweet she tasted on that very spot. A delicious compliment to the roses she always smelled of.

Fuck, right now he didn't care what happened later.

She was here now, and he was going to have her again.

And again.

CHAPTER THREE

Anna felt Blade's heated gaze, but she couldn't look at him. She'd stolen a glance right as she and Shelby rounded the corner when his attention was still on Bear. No matter how many pep talks she'd given herself since learning of this mission, she knew there'd be no preparing for when their eyes met once again. So she'd quickly looked her fill before walking fully into the room, and then focused straight ahead. Like slapping the snooze button on an alarm clock at a feeble attempt to avoid the inevitable morning, she needed just a few more minutes before getting locked in his sights. Because if she did it right now, she wasn't sure she'd be able to hide the longing she felt.

Seeing him after all these months was electrifying. Her skin sizzled, and her shallow breaths made her lightheaded. Her body knew what it wanted even when her mind screamed its protests.

"Perfect timing," Bear said, looking to them as they walked toward him. Anna leaned her hip against the table, crossed her arms to hide her tight nipples, and gave Bear her seemingly undivided attention. "I was just tellin' the guys here what's going on."

Anna nodded because she didn't trust her voice just yet.

"I haven't gotten to the specifics. Just that—"

"We have to play nice or the feds could pull the plug on our op," Gauge said.

Anna glanced at him, frowning. "What?"

"I was just telling them that, with the new FBI director, our future is in limbo."

Anna breathed a cuss word. Sure, it was a possibility that the acting director would eliminate the group after this investigation. After all, Rick wanted Shelby to investigate the members to verify loyalty, but if the guys *knew* they were being scrutinized, then it'd be that much harder to find weak spots. Anyone under a microscope would put his or her best foot forward, which would make Shelby's job more difficult. She was a young agent, and although she wasn't officially working the op alone, Anna would be busy focusing on Blade and the Mason Showalter connection. It would've been nice if Rick had actually told her he was going to put that threat out there. Now, Anna needed to do whatever she could to keep suspicion at bay so her colleague's job wouldn't be so difficult. "Yeah, well, you never really know what's going to happen when there's a changing of the guard," she said casually, as if it wasn't a real concern. Poking for more info, she glanced at Bear and asked, "Did Rick say you have to cooperate or risk dissolution?"

"Not in so many words," he said, cocking an eyebrow at her.

"He can be such an ass," Shelby muttered.

"And who are you?" Brody asked, more of a formality. Anna knew Rick had told them who'd be coming.

"Sorry, this is Shelby Landry. She's on our taskforce."

"Nice to meetcha," Brody said. Roc muttered something that could be interpreted as a greeting. Blade never took his eyes off Anna.

With introductions out of the way, Anna contemplated just how detailed Rick had been. If she confirmed their suspicions then the men would be guarded, which meant she couldn't say a darn thing about it. This added another layer of deceit because now, instead of lying by omission, she'd have to do it outright. "It's not like that."

"Then explain to me why a financial crimes task force needs hired muscle, because I gotta tell ya, I'm not terribly clear on that."

"It's not your muscle we need." She smirked and refused to think about one *muscled* man in particular standing in this room. "The IRS needs our help investigating a land buying company, so if anybody has to play nice, it's *us* with that agency."

"What the hell does the IRS have to do with the FBI?" Gauge asked.

"Besides having the same boss—i.e. the President?" She raised her eyebrow at him. Out of all the guys here, he should know how the government worked.

"Yeah, okay." Gauge half-smiled.

"They're reviewing Bartholomew Acquired Development, an entity that has taken a keen interest securing thousands of acres in Northern Louisiana." She flashed a smile. "That's our mark. We've code named them BAD, which isn't a stretch since it's the company's acronym."

"And they think the acronym is telling of the company's activities?" Gauge asked in a tone that made her think he was mentally rolling his eyes.

"No, the full name is a mouthful. Besides, you know we

love our codes. It was that or some reference to Bart Simpson. I don't have to tell you the suggestions that came up bordered on the ridiculous."

"Eat my shorts," Hunter said in a perfect Bart impression.

Anna laughed. "Exactly."

"So the IRS wants to find out if BAD is on the level," Bear said, not really asking.

She answered him anyway. "Yes. They've purchased land and mineral rights all over the U.S. Revitalizing some areas, developing others."

"That's not against the law," Roc said.

"True, but cornering a market to monopolize it is." The corner of her mouth lifted. "And so is laundering money. Oh, and tax evasion. Hence the IRS." She winked.

Even though her team was working with the SEC on this, Rick had decided it made more sense to say the IRS had instigated the investigation instead. Everyone paid taxes, and the reasoning had been it'd be easier to put the company under that agency's scrutiny than it would the SEC, which mainly focused on securities companies. Mason Showalter was an investment guy, so it made sense why he was on the SEC's radar. That excuse wouldn't work beyond that connection, though. Anna had agreed with the decision to name the IRS, although she'd been too stunned at the time to voice that.

"So BAD's been naughty," Hunter said.

"The government thinks so, which is why some of the team is in the office digging through their current holdings and back taxes and sent me out to investigate their new fascination with Louisiana."

"Tell me the code name for that is The Louisiana Purchase," Hunter said, chuckling.

Anna laughed. "No, but I'll put in the suggestion."

Bear shifted and stood. "Rick said you needed Blade for this. Why?"

That ringing in her ears was her internal alarm clock beeping, signaling the snooze-button reprieve was over. Steeling her defenses and clamping down her body's involuntary reactions, Anna looked at Blade.

And ignored the heat in his gaze he did nothing to hide.

"A Mr. Braxton Young owns shares in a privately-held company called Bayou Beasts." Blade's eyes narrowed, simmering some of the heat, and she continued. "We've learned Bayou Beasts has been approached by representatives of BAD inquiring on purchasing their land."

"So? We get approached several times a year by someone interested in buying. We ain't selling." The hard look in his eyes told her that much was true, but she was here to change that opinion. Time to get him to agree.

"The feds want you to entertain their offer."

"Fuck. That." Blade stood.

She'd expected some resistance, but his strong stance was a little shocking to her. She was prepared to follow him out the door—not willing to be alone with him just yet, but not having much of a choice. Thankfully, Brody grabbed his arm, stopping his retreat, and stood beside him. When he spoke to Anna, he was much calmer than his colleague. "Why does the government want them to sell to a company under investigation?"

"We don't, but BAD needs to believe Bayou Beasts is seriously considering it. It'd open up dialogue between the two companies, and hopefully we can learn something useful for the IRS to decide if formal charges are necessary." She looked at Blade and tilted her head to the side, readying to pry into his connection with the company. "Why wouldn't they sell? They sold to you."

Blade scoffed. "My family owns that land. I was written out of the will, but after my father died, my mom transferred my share to me. It was *her* family land anyway."

This was family land? Anna schooled her expression as emotions rioted inside her. Surely, the key players in this investigation already knew this wasn't just a business investment for Blade, but his *family*. Jeez, that meant this was personal to him. Why wasn't she told this? Granted, there was a small possibility her team wasn't aware since Mason Showalter wasn't an owner of Bayou Beasts, and he was the true mark of this investigation. Well, the SEC's investigation. Either way, she'd have to contact Rick with this news. Anna had either learned more in her brief time here than her team had realized, or she needed to chew her boss out for withholding intel. Regardless, her previous worry of betraying Blade just increased a million fold since they weren't dealing with some nameless business partners. What a mess.

"How long has it been in your family?"

"Since The Louisiana Purchase," he said, deadpan.

Hunter chuckled, and Anna cracked a smile, but she kept her focus on Blade, which was both extremely difficult and incredibly easy. "I guess it doesn't matter when they bought it, just that they have it now. This actually makes things easier. We can drive down and be directly involved in the *negotiations* instead of getting information second-hand or through surveillance." This could definitely work in their favor, which made her feel like a crappy person.

"I'm not getting my family involved."

"And you're not going anywhere!" Brody crossed his

arms, but his eyes looked almost wild. *What the hell?* "I need you here for the wedding."

"That's still months—"

Brody's gaze cut to Bear, and he cut him off by saying, "Xan's pregnant. We're moving up the wedding."

There was a chorus of congratulations and back claps. All Anna was thinking was pregnancy...wedding...distractions. None of it made any sense, but all translated into complications.

"Shit, when?" Roc asked suddenly.

Brody winced. "Sorry, man. I was gonna talk to you after the meeting. We just found out yesterday. She hasn't gone to the doc yet, but she's insisting on getting married as soon as possible. And before you say it, she's against eloping. She wants the ceremony, reception, the works."

Roc swore and looked away. His face was red, and Anna was confused by the whole exchange.

"Are you really thinking about breaking a pregnant woman's heart?" Blade asked him.

Roc growled as he ran a hand through his dark hair. "Fuck. No. Fine. Let me know when she wants to do it, and I'll make sure it's good to go."

"We'll all help you get the barn ready," Bear said.

Roc grumbled something, but Anna didn't make out his words. The tone, however, was clear. "I'll need a couple of weeks."

"That'll work." Brody looked at Bear. "Which means Blade can't go anywhere before then. I need him here. Shit's gonna be fast and furious 'till the wedding."

That would not work. At all.

"Sorry, but I need Blade on this case," Anna said, and pursed her lips. She couldn't back down from the sole reason she was here. If Blade didn't help Anna, not only was her assignment fucked, but Blade would continue to work at the garage, negating Shelby's cover reason for even being here. The upcoming nuptials threw a monkey wrench into both of the plans, so thinking quickly, she'd have to sell the argument that it was still doable. They'd just have to work around the wedding. Her gaze slid to Blade. "We can go to Louisiana and get the process rolling before you'd need to be back for the ceremony."

He looked at her like she'd grown a second head. "I'm the best man. I can't just show up right before the wedding. I have responsibilities. There's the rehearsal, the bachelor party, and the manpower needed to help get it ready in time." He shook his head. "I'm not leaving Brody to take care of this on his own." It looked like he wanted to say more, but didn't.

Crap. Very valid points. What could she say to that? If she didn't come up with a way to convince him quickly, this mission was D.O.A.

"How many days do you *have* to be in town?" She'd never planned a wedding before, but by the sounds of it, it was a local thing. Everything already planned, just moved up because of the pregnancy.

"They're supposed to get married in Roc's barn, and it's not even finished yet."

"He'll have us to help," Gauge said. Anna glanced at him, and at least he looked as if he understood the need to see the assignment through.

Bear sighed, but it was a sound of resolve that eased Anna a little before he even spoke. "We don't have a choice, man." He looked at Anna. "Can you spend a week there getting things lined out, letting his family know what's up, and then come back for a week to do wedding stuff?" He glanced at Brody. "Assuming Xan wants to do the wedding in two weeks?"

"I'll get a date locked down tonight. At this point, though, I'm thinking two weeks from Saturday will work."

Anna considered how they'd go about it if they stayed in Mayflower the week of the wedding. It would take time anyway to facilitate meetings with the company. They could go, do what they could themselves, and schedule face time with the other players for after the wedding. With technology, she wasn't even sure if in-person meetings would be necessary after their initial visit. Either way, it was doable. As long as she maintained her need to work with Blade while they were here so she could dig into the real reason she needed to be so close to him. "I don't have a problem with that."

"I do," Blade said to Brody. "I'm not leaving you, man. There's so much shit you gotta do, and knowing you, you'll try to do it all yourself and be stressed the fuck out." He looked at Anna and leveled her with the coldest stare she'd ever seen from him. In that moment, he looked deadly. "No."

"Blade," Bear barked. "What part of *we don't have a choice* do you not get?"

"We won't let him take on everything alone," Hunter said. "Within the next twenty-four hours, we'll have wedding duties divided among the rest of us. We'll all be so up in his business, he'll be sick of us."

Brody clapped Blade on the back. "I'd rather you be here, but Bear's right. We don't need to strain our relationship with the feds, and you'll be here the week leading up to it, which is when I'm likely to go apeshit anyway."

"And it might not even take us a week. Could just be a few days?" Anna said, trying to placate him.

After several tense seconds, Blade breathed, "Fine," through gritted teeth. Then, shocking Anna, he took a step toward her. Her heart raced with both anticipation and trepidation. She fought the instinct to step back. "But I'll say again, we are not involving my family. The last thing they need to worry about is some possible criminal snooping around."

She licked her dry lips. If he didn't like the first part of this, he was going to really hate what she was going to say next. "Good thing we can't tell Bayou Beasts it's a setup. We need their cooperation, but they have to believe it's all legit." Translation: he'd have to lie to his family.

"No fuckin' way. They won't ever sell." He inched closer to her. "And they're staying out of it."

"Not an option," she said, not backing down. Blade could be intimidating as hell, but she was resolved to have this work her way. Wedding wrinkle excluded. "We need them, and we can't have them slipping up and blurting the truth. You *know* how cases work. This isn't your first rodeo."

Another step toward her. "When we need the cooperation of an ally, they are usually cleared to hear the particulars of a case."

"This is a joint effort, and I've been given orders by my boss who was given orders by his. It's not as if I can call him up and argue the point. Another agency is primary with this, and I've been told no one else besides the people in this room can know. My hands are tied."

"So you expect me to lie to my family."

Yes.

She wanted to deny it, but she couldn't dig the hole of deceit any deeper. Instead, she said, "The government does." When he just stared at her, she added softly, "Some-times we have no choice." The truth of those words hurt more than she could show. She hated lying to him about anything, especially something that would destroy any hope of them exploring things further between them, assuming there was a slim chance he'd want her for something more than friends-with-benefits, a prospect she'd shielded herself from six months ago. But now even something temporary and casual was out of the question because no way would he forgive her for dragging his family into all of this. The crushing reality of their situation hurt more than she imagined was possible.

He opened his mouth and slammed it shut before storming off. She watched him walk away, angry with herself, the system, and frankly, him. It wasn't fair to put him in that category, but logic didn't have a role right now.

"Give him a few days," Bear said.

"We're already on borrowed time." Another statement laced with painful meaning.

"Give him a few days. He'll do it," Brody said, echoing their boss's words.

Anna had no choice but to wait. Blade had no choice but to help. Neither had any other option but to go down this disastrous path.

Lying to him. Dragging his family into the investigation. Lying to his family.

All to investigate a man who might be crooked that was marginally linked to Blade...which snowballed into her team having to lie to the rest of the Bang Shift so the FBI could dig into their lives to see how far Colonel's cover up went, even though they'd worked with these men on cases since that man had been exposed.

Disastrous path? That was a huge understatement.

There was no way these two combined missions wouldn't detonate a bomb in the middle of several relationships.

Professional and personal.

Very, very personal.

CHAPTER FOUR

For the last few days, Blade had growled around, ignoring snide comments about his attitude, as he tried to wrap his head about this new development that thrust the woman of his fantasies back into his life.

Anna Sue Fisher.

God, he just didn't know how to feel about all of this. He wanted her. Fucking badly. But this shit about his family? Yeah, that was a bucket of ice on his libido. He'd vacillated between being grateful circumstances had brought her back to town and being pissed off he was at the center of said circumstances. He didn't know which reaction was worse. When he was thrilled she was back, he'd been fighting wood at the shop. Not where he wanted to be when his body reacted to visions of her writhing beneath him. Later that day, new anger surged about the position this assignment was putting him in, and he'd lashed out, going so far as to suggest one of the other guys work with her. And not just any guy. He'd actually suggest Roc.

Fucking Roc!

Hunter had even expressed some positive points about

Roc going instead of Blade, but everyone knew he'd only said those things because he wanted that man as far away from his sister as possible.

Brody had yanked Blade to the side and told him to knock it off. He was in a bad way if he'd rather Roc not only interact with his family but also work closely with Anna. Jesus, *Roc*. Out of all the guys at the shop and in the crew, he was the most ruthless, the most calculating. The most lethal...and that was saying something since Blade had actually killed before.

Yeah, Blade seriously wasn't thinking straight at all when it came to Anna Sue and this whole fucked up situation.

So Blade had relented, given up the fight, and accepted this damn assignment, which was why he was now sitting in the driveway of Anna Sue's house waiting for her ass to get out here. This had been the same house she'd lived in when she was here as extra eyes on Xan. A house that hadn't been hers after all. It was an FBI safe house, a house she now shared with Shelby and would flee from again once her job was done.

Blade honked for the second time. A dick move, but he'd be damned if he went to her door like this was some kind of date. Besides, he had a lot of things he wanted to say to her, and if he went into the house, he'd get an audience for this speech. Nope, he needed stay in the SUV and wait for her. He also didn't need to jump right into any serious conversation the moment he saw her. He took a calming breath. He'd waited six months. He could wait a little bit longer.

By the time Anna came out, he was almost back to his senses. Almost. She was laughing at something Shelby said as the fellow agent walked with her to his vehicle. Not that he paid the other woman any attention. Hell, he couldn't even look at Anna's face. She had on the tiniest pair of shorts and a skin-tight tank top. *Fuuuuck.*

The night they'd been together he'd spent a lot of time remembering every inch of her creamy thighs before feeling them wrapped around him. And now he had a gorgeous view of those legs.

"We need to go if we want to get there before dark," he said, barely checking the edge in his voice he'd just spent several minutes trying to ease.

Anna's gaze cut to his. "I know." Then she looked at Shelby again, effectively cutting him off. "Call me if you need anything." She tossed her bags in the back of the SUV.

"Will do," Shelby said. "Be safe." They hugged before Anna closed the back door and opened the passenger one. She slid in as Shelby waved at him. He gave her a quick nod and put the car in reverse, ready to be done with the good-byes and on the damn road. Before he said anything else, Anna pulled out a rabbit ear keychain and hung it around the rearview.

"Surprised you still do that," he snapped. Back in Dallas, he'd thought it cute when she hung rabbit ears from the rearview mirror. He'd even joked that she must have a case of them back home. She'd defended that they weren't real rabbit's feet, but the good-luck gesture made her feel safer. Silly, yes. But he hadn't been about to look at a rabbit-foot keychain since then and not think of her. "Figured your luck ran out a long time ago."

"What's up your ass?" Anna asked him as he scowled at the road like it owed him money.

"You are. This whole situation is." He forced himself to take a deep breath and calm his anger. Again. Anger at this mission. Anger at how beautiful she was. At how close she sat next to him. Practically naked. The attitude wouldn't get him anywhere with her. Where was the happy-go-lucky persona he'd spent years building?

Probably panting at this woman's feet.

She sighed. "I know. I'm not happy about it either."

And the thing was, he believed her. It disarmed him a little more...until he questioned why she wasn't happy with this assignment. Did she not like bringing his family into this, or did she not like being here with him? Either was possible. Neither brought the same response out of him.

They had a long ride ahead of themselves. If he wanted answers, it wasn't as if she couldn't get away from him. He'd preferred to gently start this conversation after they'd had a moment to adjust being in the car. But fuck it. There was no time like the present.

"You disappeared after Dallas."

She sucked in air. "You don't pull punches, do you?" she muttered, looking out the passenger window.

Blade waited, the seconds ticking by in silence. When it became apparent she wasn't going to comment on her own, he decided to turn that statement into a question with just one word. "Why?"

"Brax," she breathed, and fuck, his dick twitched. Rarely anybody called him by his given name. Even his family called him Blade. Anna Sue did too, the exception being when they'd made love that night. Hearing her call him that brought very specific memories flooding back.

"Babe, it's a simple question."

Her gaze narrowed when she trained it on him. "Because I didn't want to become just another Blade Bimbo."

"What the hell does that mean?" he asked, the clipped tone back.

"You know damn well that I mean. When it comes to

women, you flirt and fuck. When was the last time you had a real relationship?"

"I'm an adult, and the women I've been with have been consenting adults. I very clearly recall you being more than just consenting. I distinctly remember you—"

"Stop." Her hand flew up as if her saying the command wasn't enough. "My point is, you have a track record of sleeping around. I don't. Our ideals don't mesh. Plus, we work together. If I were to ignore what I need for great sex, I'd be the one to get hurt when you've had your fill and are ready to move onto the next flavor of the week."

"You don't think very highly of me, do you?" he asked, pissed that she was both right and wrong about him. Yes, he slept around, but that didn't mean he was opposed to the idea of a relationship. He just never felt good enough for someone. And the truth was, he'd never be good enough for Anna. He avoided relationships because he wasn't worthy, not because he preferred being a man whore.

"I think very highly of you, actually." He felt her eyes on him again, his skin heating at her admission, and he couldn't help but steal another glance. "We just want different things. Doesn't mean I didn't wish things could be different. It is what it is." She shrugged as if everything was as simple as that. She wasn't wrong, just incorrect in the reasoning behind it.

They drove in silence as they ate up the miles, but his mind was anything but quiet. After some time, he asked, "Is that your only hang up?" Because he clearly didn't know how to accept rejection and just let it go.

She quirked an eyebrow. "Well, I am in law enforcement and you're a mercenary. We may play well together during recess, but I have no idea what you do when class is back in session."

He chuckled at her analogy. "Your agency doesn't seem to have a problem with it."

She glanced away, but not before he caught a troubled look in her eyes. "What?"

"You told me you were arrested," she said without looking at him. Was she avoiding answering him? She wasn't technically changing the subject, but her statement felt like a diversionary tactic.

"And?"

Anna shifted in her seat so that she faced him fully. "You never said why. Feels like you have secrets, and I'm not talking of the I-stole-Uncle-Billy Bob's-car-and-took-it-joyriding variety. Your secrets feel like red flags."

Well, fuck. He did have secrets. One in particular he could never tell another living soul. "I don't have an Uncle Billy Bob," he said to stall.

"I wouldn't know that either," she said softly.

"You're right. My life isn't an open book. I have my reasons." He clenched the steering wheel tighter. He did have his reasons, and most centered around a very big one.

"Why were you arrested?"

And that was the biggie.

He glared at her before answering the question he hated she uttered. Hated because he couldn't lie to her. Not that he could tell her everything. "Murder."

Anna paled.

Blade sighed. "The charges didn't stick. It was the only time I'd ever been arrested. Other than that fucked up situation, I've practically been a model citizen." He smiled what he hoped was his dazzling one that got him whatever he wanted from the opposite sex, and what he wanted from her right now was to accept his answer and leave it at that. He hadn't lied. He'd been arrested for Jeremiah's murder, but without evidence—or a body—Blade's lawyer nipped that shit in the bud.

Unfortunately, there was no statute of limitations on murder. He'd never be able to tell anyone what really happened that night. Not only could he risk loyalties changing, but he also wouldn't risk the wrong person getting wind of what he'd done. A confession would get him a pair of matching bracelets and a murder sentence. Even if he was careful, there was always the risk he'd be charged again. One of the few things Colonel had done for him was get rid of the arrest record and whatever evidence there was against him. But that didn't mean cases couldn't be built again. Nor did it mean that Colonel never talked to someone else. There were too many questions out there. It was better for him to live life alone. He couldn't plant himself in a woman's life, knowing there was a chance he'd be ripped from it. No, all he could promise a woman was temporary companionship. It was a rule he'd lived by because anything more was too dangerous.

Too painful.

Especially when he weighed the options of changing that life rule for Anna Sue, and the risks glared back, mocking him.

"Charges being dropped isn't the same thing as being innocent," she said, ripping him from his musings, replacing any sad feelings of resolve with another harsh reality.

She was a cop. And fuck, he should've known she'd pick up on his word choice. No way was he talking about this. He wasn't lying to her and he wasn't going to open up either. She was too sharp. He had zero answers for her, so he did the next best thing. Pushed the focus onto her. "Spoken like a true detective. So tell me something, Agent Fisher. When was the last time *you* had a real relationship?"

As more miles burned, he realized, he wasn't the only one who didn't have answers to give.

————

"WHEN WAS the last time you had a real relationship?"

He'd nailed the hammer straight on the head with that question, effectively shutting down their conversation.

Anna Sue hadn't had a boyfriend since college, and even that one only lasted about six months. Her dream had been to become an FBI agent. She'd worked hard, always having her nose in a book or ass at the shooting range. She'd focused on forensic accounting...but most men who applied to the bureau relied on their law enforcement backgrounds and criminal justice degrees. She'd done her research early on and had learned if she wanted a real shot at making agent, she'd need to bring something extra to the table. She went the nerd route, majoring in accounting and minoring in a highly sought-after foreign language while spending her valuable free time training for the physical aspects of the job.

Men had been a luxury she couldn't afford. Oh, she'd dreamed about having a man in her life. One who'd support her career and love her in spite of her dedication to it. But the reality was, she still didn't have time to find such a man.

As the hours passed, Anna kept drifting back to Blade turning her question around on her. Not only had he touched on a sore subject, making her want to justify her life, but it also made her realize that maybe she'd done the same thing when posing the question to him in the first place. She felt judgey, which made her feel even worse. Torn between defending herself and lashing out at him, she'd kept her mouth closed instead.

Every so often Blade would start up benign conversation, and Anna would contribute until it died down and more silence ensued. If it wasn't for the lingering unanswered questions on both their parts from their initial *major* conversation, the silence would have been compatible. Instead, it felt thick, heavy with declarations and demands that refused to be expressed. The closer they got to the state border, the tenser things felt in the car. They hadn't stopped in a while. Her ankle was cramping and her shoulders were stiff from the stress. What she wouldn't give for a long bath—

"Look out!" she yelled, grabbing the dash as they rounded a corner. Something metal lay in the road. Blade swerved, but caught the edge of it.

"*Shit.*" The tire popped, and the vehicle bounced to the side. Blade yanked it onto the shoulder of the road, and they came to a bumpy stop. "Are you okay?"

She took a deep breath, her heart racing like crazy with the sudden adrenaline. "Yeah."

He hopped out, and Anna followed, knowing he wouldn't want the excess weight in the vehicle when he changed the tire. "What was it?" she asked when she got to the back of the SUV.

"Looks like a crowbar." He picked it up and tossed it into the ditch.

"How the hell did a crowbar slash the tire?"

Blade walked to the bad tire and squatted. "Looks like it didn't. It caught between the tire and the wheel. Separated the two." He sighed as he stood. "It'll have to be remounted." Without looking at her, he made his way to the back of the SUV and started moving their bags to the back seat. Anna considered grabbing her own bags, but Blade managed to move them all before her brain caught up with what he was doing—getting the spare. Not that she felt bad. It was a little karma for him honking at her earlier and not offering to help when he picked her up. Petty? A little.

"Fuck!"

Anna jumped. "What?"

"There's not a goddamn jack."

"Are you *kidding* me?"

He slammed the back door and whirled. "Do I look like I'm kidding?"

"You're a mechanic. Isn't there some law that says you're supposed to do things like check oil and fluid levels, and oh, I don't know, make sure there's a fucking spare and shit in the back before road trips?" It wasn't fair for her to take this out on him, but come on! He. Was. A. Mechanic.

Glaring, he said, "I changed the oil yesterday and topped off all the fluids. Fuck, I even washed and vacuumed it."

"Just didn't double check on the spare."

"We have a spare," he gritted out. "Fucking Roc." He stormed to the front of the vehicle. "Asshole borrowed the jack the other day because he couldn't wait on Brody to finish with the one at the shop. My truck was closest. I forgot." He grabbed his cellphone and made a call while she walked away. She had no idea where they were at. They'd passed a gas station and motel a few miles back, but they were currently on a two-lane highway with nothing but trees as far as the eye could see. Who knew how close they were to an actual town?

"Tow truck will take a couple of hours. We can either wait here, or walk back to the motel and check in for the night."

It was hot and she had on sandals.

But they'd get to the hotel faster than the tow truck got

to them, and frankly, she didn't feel like sitting here with nothing to do other than chitchat with Blade.

"Let me get my laptop case and small bag." She could leave her main suitcase with her clothes, but she would want a shower as soon as they checked in and could just put on her PJs that she had in that smaller bag. As for her laptop? She never left her FBI issued computer unattended.

Blade strapped his long duffle bag over his shoulder and grabbed her bigger suitcase.

"That one can stay. I just need my smaller one."

He didn't say anything as he handed over her laptop case. She slung it over her shoulder with her purse as he took her smaller bag and propped it on top of the larger case, wrapping the straps around the extended handle, securing them together. Without another word, he reached for her laptop and pried it off her shoulder.

"Hey, I can carry that."

He sighed as he pulled the strap of her case over his head and across his chest. "I know you can. Just let me, please." He looked like he'd aged ten years in ten minutes, and she felt like total shit. The tire thing wasn't his fault, but he was carrying the blame just like he was carrying her bags.

"I'm sorry. I didn't mean to say that earlier," she said softly, reaching out and stroking his arm. It was the first time she'd touched him since she'd been back, and she had to stop herself from stepping up against him and wrapping her arms around his back.

He stepped away and started walking down the road. "We'll go slow, so you don't hurt your ankle," he said tenderly.

Anna Sue wanted to cry in that moment. She'd been a bitch to him, and he was worried about her. It made all the issues between them seem so insignificant. If he was another man and she another woman, they could be laughing about this little mishap, making lifelong memories. Instead, they both wanted each other on some level; maybe not the same level, but there was definite want on both sides. Yet, no matter their feelings, it could never be. Not really.

Lies, deceit.

Lust, tenderness.

Anna Sue was more confused about this man now than she was a week ago, and as they made their way slowly to the motel, Blade glancing at her ankle every so often, she knew that said confusion would only grow and make things even more difficult between them.

CHAPTER FIVE

Anna Sue had sweat rolling down her neck, but as much as Blade wanted to fantasize about how salty her skin would taste right this second, he was too worried about her messing up her ankle to even go there. Her injury had happened over six months ago, but it had freaked him out then, and worried him still. Sure, she seemed healed, but he hated putting her through this kind of strain.

"Almost there, babe," he said for the third time since the motel came into view.

"Brax, I'm fine," she said, a little exasperation in her voice. He'd smile at her tone if he wasn't concerned about her ankle. Logically, he knew she would've had to be cleared by the feds before going back into the field, but his reaction was born out of something more primal and less logical.

And when she called him by his real name? That primal instinct revved up even higher, although it wasn't so much sexual need as a need to take care of her.

Fuck, he was so damn irritated with himself over the car jack. When he got back to the shop, he was going to kick

Roc's ass over this, but the final blame fell on Blade. He should have double-checked it along with everything else before hitting the road. Hell, he didn't even make sure his emergency kit was still back there. He just assumed it was just like he'd done the jack. It *was* back there. He'd seen it when searching for his nonexistent jack, but still. He should have made sure before leaving.

When they finally reached the front door to the motel, he breathed a sigh of relief. "Sit down," he said, pointing to a bench by the front desk. She didn't argue.

Blade made fast work booking a two-bed room. As soon as he got the keys, he walked to the bench and grabbed her hand, pulling her up.

"I told you I'm fine."

He grunted and led her back out of the lobby and down the sidewalk to their room.

"Jeez, it's hot in here," Anna said when they walked in. The air was definitely stifling in the cramped space, so he dropped her bags and made a beeline to the thermostat.

"I'm going to take a cold shower," she said, not looking at him as she walked into the bathroom.

Blade kicked off his shoes and stood in front of the air vent to cool off, trying his damnedest not to think about Anna undressing in the next room.

Or her all wet when he heard the shower turn on.

Or her rubbing soapy hands all over her body.

He cussed softly, ordering his thoughts not to go there and his dick to go back down. It wasn't as if anything changed between them. If anything, they were solidified in the hands-off category after their talk in the car. Not that it changed his feeling about her.

Feelings?

Hell, he didn't know what to call it. He liked her as a person. Wanted her sexually. He knew he'd been obsessed with her since their mission in Dallas, and never before had a woman dominated his thoughts. Yeah, he had feelings for her. He was man enough to admit that…and too much of a chicken-shit to analyze just how deep those feeling ran. Why? Because there wasn't a damn thing he could do about it. If anything, it should make him want to avoid her even more. Keep from hurting her down the road when his past caught up with him.

He hoped that day would never come, but it was better to plan for the worst and hope for the best. Anna Sue's heart wasn't something he was willing to chance.

By the time the water shut off and he heard the bath-room door open, he'd gotten his libido under control. He turned to face her, and sucked in all the air in the room.

The only thing on her body was a thin towel. Water beaded on her shoulders, her hair hanging in wet curls. She was fucking beautiful.

His gaze traced her movements as she made her way to her bag and pulled out some lotion. The moment she opened it, his senses were assaulted with that beautiful rose scent she always smelled of.

"I, er, wanted to apologize again for what I said to you after the tire incident," she said, not looking at him.

"Don't worry about it," he said hoarsely, and cleared his throat. "It's been a stressful day."

"No excuse." She glanced up at him.

"Then you're forgiven." Because he didn't want to think about his screw up, nor did he want to talk about it. Since she'd stopped rummaging for clothes to bring it up, the fastest way to get her back on task was to agree.

Because he needed her fucking dressed before he did

something stupid. Like rip that flimsy towel off and kiss her everywhere.

She sighed and stood fully. Blade turned to inspect the air conditioning unit, needing some kind of distraction. He heard her moving and was immediately grateful she apparently went back to getting dressed.

Until she stood beside him, still wet and covered in that sorry-excuse-for-a-towel.

"You need to get dressed," he gritted out.

"I was such a bitch to you."

He grabbed her arms. To keep her away? To pull her closer? He had no freaking idea. He held her still as his conflicting desires warred. "I'm not easily offended, babe." Hell, he didn't even know if that was true. His mouth was just rambling stuff as a distraction to his carnal instincts.

"I'm sorry," she said softly, and damn if he didn't want to haul her against him and kiss her until the sadness in her eyes evaporated.

"It's okay," he murmured.

She rose up on her toes, and he had a second to understand what she was doing. He opened his mouth to say something to stop her, but it was too late. Her lips glanced his. He stifled a groan as she captured his lower lip between hers and fisted his hands to keep from tugging her towel off.

As quickly as the kiss started, it stopped. She cleared her throat as she lowered down to her regular height. She smiled tentatively and walked around him. He turned to watch her, and she, thankfully—or frustratingly—pulled out clothes and ducked into the bathroom. When she was out of sight, he let out the breath he'd been holding.

It was just a friendly kiss. Don't think too much about it.

Yeah, right. His cock refused to hear reason.

When she came back out, she didn't seem as affected by it as he was.

Anna pulled her suitcase off the bed closest to the door. "I'm taking this one since your safety is my responsibly, and I'm the one with the gun." She winked.

He laughed, walking over to her. Rather than take his bag off the bed she was cleaning off and claiming, he picked up her bags and tossed them on the other bed. "Not happening, babe. I get door duty."

Her hand flew to her chest in mock offense. "What, you don't like having your body protected by a girl?"

"Darlin', you can do anything to my body at anytime." He leaned closer, her eyes dilating. Hmmm...she wasn't as unaffected by him as she pretended to be. "But my ass is sleeping by the door."

"You're pushy," she said without malice as she moved to the other bed.

"I'm sorry, babe, but your safety isn't something I'll ever relent on."

Without another word, she crawled into bed.

Now, it was his turn for a cold shower. A very cold shower.

———

ANNA SUE and Blade pulled up to a huge set of gates, the iron an intricate artwork possessing an image of an alligator spanning across both doors.

"Wow," she breathed as the doors opened.

Blade didn't say anything about her surprise of the beautiful lands. Lands that had been in his family for generations.

Family she was only minutes away from meeting.

Butterflies were kickboxing each other in her stomach. Normally when she worked a case, she didn't get nervous, but this wasn't normal. At all.

When they'd gotten up this morning, Blade had seemed tense. She'd at first blamed it on her impromptu kiss last night. She still didn't understand what had come over her. She'd felt so bad about blaming him for their predicament and wanted to do *something* to make it up to him. But kiss?

The fact that she'd spent part of her shower remembering the last time she was near him *and* in a shower hadn't helped. That night, Blade had opened the door in all his naked glory with the intent of getting clean. He did, after getting extra dirty. That man had picked her up and fucked her against the wall as water sluiced off his magnificent body. That image last night had forced her out of her shower much faster than she'd planned. She hadn't had enough time to get her emotions under control. Her skin had been too hot to get dressed, and coupled with her yearning for him was lingering shame of how she'd talked to him on the side of the road. So she'd ended up kissing him.

And immediately stopping.

It hadn't been a good idea, but she didn't regret it. Just that little taste of him was like one smoke for an addict. She wanted more, wanted to suck him in and never breathe him out. She had no other choice but to stop before it really got started.

But he'd seemed fine last night, if not a little stunned. He hadn't lashed out or anything; in fact, he'd been playful. But when they'd gotten up this morning, tension radiated off him. This feeling seemed deeper, meaningful. She just wasn't privy to that meaning, and he hadn't opened up. Even seeing his SUV had been dropped off early that morning and the keys waiting for them at the front desk hadn't eased his mood. He hadn't said much on the ride over either. Well, other than to clarify their cover story.

And *that* was another matter entirely. She knew they'd have to come up with a reason for her being here with him, but she had a dozen options on the ready. Her favorite? She was his accountant—because she was one—here to help him evaluate the offer on the table from BAD. Because there was one. The best lies were the ones closest to the truth.

He'd said it was his family, so his choice.

She hadn't argued. Partly because she'd been too tongue-tied to voice her objection.

"It's so pretty out here," she said, glancing around to look out all the windows.

He finally smiled for the first time this morning. "Yeah. It's peaceful. For the most part." Then the smile was gone and something dark briefly clouded his eyes. He blinked as if to push away whatever bad thoughts encroached on his mind.

"What? Except all the alligators?" she said, joking.

He snorted and glanced at her. "Yeah, the gators screw up the serenity."

"But they make you money."

"That they do." He winked at her, and she was relieved his mood seemed to be lightening, if only a little.

They pulled into a huge circle drive of an enormous plantation- style house. Seriously, the columns were huge and went all the way around the house. "Holy shit," she breathed.

"Yeah, my great-great-great grandfather built it. Nice, huh?"

"It's insane."

He pulled to a stop by the massive front porch and got out. Anna was still a little stunned and she didn't get out right away. When Blade opened the car door for her, she startled. "Oh, sorry."

He smiled and offered his hand to help her get out. She took it automatically, but quickly released it when she exited. She opened her mouth to thank him when the front door of the house whooshed opened and someone squealed.

"Blade! My baby!"

A tiny woman with dark blonde hair came running down the stairs and flew into his arms.

"Momma," he said softly, hugging her tightly. When he pulled away, his smile glowed as he stared down at her. "How are you?"

She waved him away. "Fine, fine." Then she glanced at Anna and smiled. "Are you going to introduce me?" She'd asked him, but her gaze stayed locked on Anna.

Blade stepped back so that he stood next to her and put a hand on her lower back, the move possessive and definitive. Even though she knew what was coming, those butterflies were back with a vengeance. Maybe if he hadn't just told her this morning just how he was going to explain Anna to his family, she wouldn't be as nervous.

Because she was seriously freaking out on the inside. She needed more time to come to terms with the cover story.

"Momma, this is Anna Sue. My fiancée."

Yep, definitely needed more time. Like, maybe a year or two.

"What?"

Now, Anna was a trained FBI agent. She could deflect an attack and take down an assailant with no warning. Seriously, she'd made grown men twice her size cry in agony in under three seconds flat when they'd tried to surprise her, but when this tiny woman lunged and wrapped Anna in her arms, she'd been shocked frozen.

"Momma, let her go," Blade said with a chuckle. The woman held onto her tighter.

"No way."

"C'mon, Mom, you gotta—are you crying?" he asked incredulously.

"No."

Yes, she was. Tears dripped onto Anna's bare shoulder. Anna stared at Blade over the woman's head and begged him with her gaze to do something.

His shrug told her he couldn't do anything about it.

Anna's returning glare told him there'd be payback.

Finally, he tugged on his mom until she released him.

"Oh, lordy, where are my manners? I'm Bernadette Young."

"It's a pleasure to meet you, Mrs. Young."

"None of that, dear. Call me Mom."

Anna Sue blanched.

"Mother," Blade said softly. "Don't scare her off before I get a ring on her finger."

Her mom glanced down at her left hand. And Anna wanted to groan. When Blade told her this was going to be their cover story, she'd asked why a girlfriend wouldn't be enough. He'd told her that his family was very private, and he'd never brought a girl home before. For it to work, things had to seem serious between them. He couldn't very well introduce her as his wife, because he'd said his mother would kill him for getting married without her. Fiancée, it was. And she was now in Hell disguised as the state of Louisiana.

Mrs. Young grabbed Anna's hand and glared at her son.

"Braxton Beauregard Young, where is her engagement ring?"

He exhaled slowly. "I was going to talk to you about that," he said softly to his mom. Yet another part of the cover story that convinced Anna that Blade might be the devil incarnate.

Mrs. Young squealed again and wrapped Blade in another hug. "Yes, of course!" she said, knowing without further explanation that Blade was asking to use his grand-mother's engagement ring. He'd spent half the morning explaining this to Anna, but his mom understood right away.

Yep, the man wanted his pretend fiancée to wear a family heirloom to seal the fake deal. No doubt about it. This was Hell, and Blade was the devil.

"Well, c'mon," Mrs. Young said excitedly, practically dragging Anna into the house, her beloved son all but forgotten, but Blade trailed right behind them anyway.

Anna stifled a gasp as they walked into the grand foyer.

"This house has been in our family for generations."

"Brax told me."

She smiled at the mention of Blade's name. "I haven't heard anyone call him that since he was a teen. That boy was the best at taking down a gator with only a knife. His uncles started calling him that, and it eventually stuck."

"Oh, I usually call him Blade, too," she said, stumbling over her words. Was it wrong to call him Brax? When she'd done it the night they'd slept together, it was as if she'd reached right into his chest and touched his heart. She'd loved that reaction. She hadn't planned on calling him Brax again, but it had slipped and he still seemed to love hearing it from her. Did it hold more meaning for him? Should she refrain from calling him that and just stick to the name everyone used now?

"It's okay, babe." He kissed the top of her head. "You're the only one who'll get away with it."

"Awww, that's so precious," his mother said, sporting another huge grin. At this rate, she'd have premature smile lines all over her face. The lady squealed again and walked even faster up, up, and up the stairs, down a long hall, around a corner and another hall to a closed door. When Mrs. Young tugged her in, this time Anna suppressed her gasp at how beautiful the bedroom was.

Mrs. Young stepped up to a picture on a wall and pulled it out. A safe was hidden behind it. Anna swallowed, trying to get salvia back into her dry throat. Once the safe was opened, Mrs. Young grabbed a ring box and locked the safe. When she pulled it out of the box, Anna only caught a glimpse of it, but from what she could see, the thing was huge.

Blade's mom clasped his hand and dropped the ring in his palm before curling his fingers around it. "I'm so proud of you," she said softly. "I never thought you'd allow your-self to find true happiness."

Anna was going to be sick.

Blade smiled warmly at his mom and then turned to Anna. He lifted her left hand.

Anna's breath stopped.

It's not real. It's not real. It's not real.

And the love shining in his eyes was definitely *not real.* If she said it enough times, maybe she'd believe it.

"Anna," he breathed.

"I thought you said her name was Anna Sue?"

"Mom," Blade muttered through the corner of his mouth, fighting a smile as his gaze stayed locked on Anna.

He took a deep breath and started again. "Anna, from the moment you came into my life, you turned my world upside down, shattering everything I thought I knew about love. I hadn't known my soul was lost until it found its mate in you. Will you marry me?"

Stunned.

Where was the air in this room? Her lungs burned for it.

"You already said yes, babe. No take backs," he said with a smirk when she didn't immediately respond.

She blinked a few times. Those were not tears. Please don't let them be tears. "Yes," she whispered.

He smiled like she'd made him the happiest man on the planet with that one simple word. She felt him slip the ring on her finger, but she couldn't take her eyes off his face. Once it was in place, he cupped her cheeks and brushed his lips over hers. She sucked in air, and he took the opportunity to deepen the kiss. The crazy nerves swimming through her system immediately transformed into molten lava. He kissed her like he couldn't get close enough, with everything he had.

He slowly pulled away, and she groaned in frustration. He chuckled a little and tucked her hair behind her ear while her eyelids stayed shut. When she opened them, the spell would be broken, and she wanted to believe it for a few more seconds.

"That was the sweetest thing I've ever seen," his mom cooed.

Anna's eyes flew open. They weren't alone, and he'd just kissed her like a man starved right in front of his mother. Her face heated. Blade pulled her into his chest and hugged her. "Mom, we still have to check into our hotel. Do you want to meet us for lunch before we come back?"

"You will do no such thing."

"Didn't realize you were that opposed to eating."

"Son, you will stay here."

"No," he said sharply.

Anna extracted herself from his embrace, but Blade left an arm around her shoulders.

"We're going to be in town a lot. I told you, I gotta meet with other family while I'm here. There are some things going down that we all need to discuss, but it's more convenient to stay out there than drive back and forth to meet everyone."

"I already called a family meeting for this afternoon, so I will not have that staying in town business. I haven't seen you in forever."

"It's been four months," he said. The eye-roll was implied.

"It's been seventeen weeks and three days, and I wouldn't have cared even if you were here last week. This is your home. You always stay here." She turned to leave, but said over her shoulder, "I'll have Maurice change the sheets. Go get your bags."

Blade groaned as she left, but from the relaxed stance of his shoulders, Anna knew he wasn't going to push the issue with his mom. "C'mon. Let's get our stuff."

"This wasn't part of the plan," she muttered. It was bad enough they had to lie to his family about the business stuff and apparently lie about being engaged, but now they had to stay on the property and not get a break from the ruse?

"Sorry." Although he didn't sound the least bit upset about this change, too. They walked back out to the SUV. She grabbed her laptop case, and Blade secured everything else as he'd done when they'd walked to the motel yesterday. Without a word, she trekked behind him back up the stairs and around the same halls as before. "This is the family wing of the house."

"Isn't the whole house the family wing?"

He chuckled. "No. The first two floors are guest suites. Gator season doesn't last long, and those rooms are booked years in advance. We also get hunters during deer season, which usually book a year in advance. The rest of the year, it operates as a bed and breakfast, except during summer when it's closed to the public."

"Why close if it's so successful?" Her business degree was kicking in. Being closed for months every year was leaving income on the table.

"For extended family to vacation here and to schedule repairs and maintenance without interrupting guests. Plus, it's right before gator season, so it's the perfect time to spruce everything up to get ready for the new operating year."

"Ah, that makes sense."

He opened a door down the hall from the room they were in earlier. This one was smaller and more masculine. Not as outlandishly done, but still elegant. He dropped their bags by the closet as she lowered her laptop bag on the desk. Her left hand felt noticeably heavier than her right, but she still hadn't had the courage to peek at the ring.

"So, one bed," she said, stating the obvious.

"Yep. Sorry. I really thought she wouldn't fuss about me staying in town."

She could sleep in the same bed as him. They were adults.

Adults who'd had sex the last time they were in the same bed together.

But still...adults.

"She seems really, um, friendly."

He laughed. "Yeah, you'd think. But don't let that fool you. If you cross her, she'd cut you and not break a sweat."

"Great. So when she figures out this is a big fat lie, I'll have a contract on my head," Anna said, frowning. That was just what she needed. One pissed off little woman gunning for her.

Blade's smile slipped. "Don't worry about it. I won't let you take the fall," he murmured as he got closer to her. He cleared his throat when he reached her. "You haven't looked at the ring."

"It's not real," she said, looking away from him.

"I beg to differ, darlin'. It's very real."

She huffed out a partial laugh at what he was saying, and decided to lift her hand to get a look at it. She didn't want to be rude, after all.

"That's not what I mean—oh. My. God." It was huge. Like carats. It was a teardrop shape with round diamonds all around the massive stone. "I can't wear this." It was bad enough she knew he wanted her to wear something that belonged to his family, but this was too much. "It's like eleventy carats! You can buy a house with this thing."

"Possibly," he said casually. "Well, not *this* house."

"Blade, I'm serious. I already feel bad about this whole thing. I can't risk losing something like this."

"Then don't lose it," he said with a shrug. "My mom and everybody in my family probably expects my future wife to wear that ring. It helps solidify the cover. I'll have to meet with my mom, aunt, and cousins since they're all part owners. You'll be there. If you're wearing something from a mall jewelry store, it won't seem real to them. If it doesn't seem real, they won't take what you have to say seriously."

"Blade," she said, breathing, looking down at the ring. It seemed as if with every passing day the hole of lies just keeps getting bigger and bigger. She already knew she'd never escape its depths unscathed, but at this rate, she'd get buried alive.

"Anna, it's okay. Really."

"But what about your future wife? She won't like you making a mockery of her ring."

He didn't say anything, and when she looked up, he gazed into nothingness, seemingly lost in thought. When he looked at her, he didn't say anything else about it. Instead, he said, "Let's go downstairs and find something to eat. At least Mom got everyone to come here this afternoon. Maybe we won't need to be here all week after all. Figure it'd take days to gather everybody and get on their schedules. She actually saved us time without even realizing it."

She nodded, though she didn't think she'd be able to eat anything right now.

Jesus, when his mother and family learned the truth that Blade and Anna were not getting married, they'd hate her for getting Blade—and his family—mixed up in all of this.

Earlier, she'd thought Blade was the devil in her hell, but if there was an evil incarnate in this scenario, it wasn't the man disturbing his family life under the guise of helping the government. He was just an innocent man who got sucked into all of this

No, if there was a devil here, she wore sandals and a rock the size of a prize-winning ear of corn on her left ring finger.

CHAPTER SIX

WHEN ANNA WALKED out of the en suite bathroom later that afternoon, having showered and changed into something more conservative—her words, not his—Blade almost swallowed his tongue. When he didn't think she could be any more beautiful, she surprised him again and again. Capri slacks, heels, almost sheer blouse.

And his grandma's engagement ring. His chest tightened at the sight of it on her finger. He liked it way more than he should. When he told her about his plan, he'd almost laughed at how big her eyes had gotten. He knew when he'd mentioned having a family ring she'd wear she had no idea just what he had in store for her. The only reason he felt comfortable with it being out of a locked safe was because he knew it was insured. Granted, it held more sentimental value than any monetary one placed on it, but still. If something awful happened to the ring, they were covered.

"You look beautiful." He rocked back on his heels and pushed his hands into his pockets to keep from reaching for her.

"Thanks. You look nice, too." Blade had changed into some jeans and a short-sleeved button-down. He hadn't showered again since, once the meeting was over, he intended on going out and walking around some of the property. It'd take days to scout everything, so he'd start today to make sure he covered everything. And there was one spot in particular he wouldn't put off going to.

"You ready to head down? They should be here in about twenty minutes."

"Yeah. I need to check in with Rick sometime," she said as she grabbed her cellphone and walked toward him near the door.

"How long do you need?" he asked softly before opening the door.

"Probably ten minutes. Not long."

He nodded and opened the door. "You can go outside and call when we get down there."

They walked down to the first floor, and he placed his hand on the small of her back to guide her into the den.

"Jesus, are there any small rooms in this house?"

"We don't do small, sweetie," his mom said.

He turned toward her, tugging Anna with him. "Enjoy your nap?"

"Of course. I think everyone should sleep for an hour in the middle of the day. Keeps you young." She giggled.

"You have a very beautiful home, Mrs. Young."

His mom tsked. "I told you to call me Mom." At Blade's glare, his mom added, "Or Bernadette, but none of this *Mrs. Young* business. Makes me feel old."

"You don't look a day over thirty."

His mother beamed. "I knew I liked her."

"She's likable," Blade said as he gently rubbed circles on her back.

His mom clasped her hands together. "Okay, a quick family lesson. Come over here." She walked to the side of the room where several photos were on display. She pointed out generations of grandparents, aunts, uncles, and cousins.

"Here's Blade in his wild days." She chuckled.

"Just because I rode a motorcycle with a group of friends doesn't mean I was in a gang." Blade practically rolled his eyes with that statement.

Anna bent over and got a closer look. "You were adorable." She smiled up at him.

"I was badass." He narrowed his eyes playfully.

"Language," his mother muttered before she continued on pointing out various family members within the collage. When she got to the family photo taken when Blade was even younger, he stiffened.

"...And here's Blade again. Younger than his biker days. Wasn't he so cute? That's me and his dad. And that right here was his sister, Brenna." His mom's voice held a touch of sadness, and he knew it wouldn't escape Anna's keen observation.

Anna leaned her head against Blade's chest and wrapped her arms around his waist. He instinctively wound his arms around her, holding her. "She was a beautiful girl." He hadn't missed her use of the past tense, which meant she caught on that his sister was no longer alive.

Blade held her tighter, and said, "Yeah, she was." He dropped his head to her hair and kissed her. "Don't you have to check in back home, babe?"

She nodded against him before pulling away. "Sorry," she said to his mom. "I was supposed to call and let them know we made it okay yesterday, but after the flat tire debacle, I totally forgot. I'll just be a few minutes."

"Oh, no worries, sweetie."

Blade pointed to the French doors at the other end of the room. "You can go out there and make it. It won't be too hot in the shade."

"No alligators on the porch, are there?" she asked with a quirked eyebrow and a small smile.

"No, smarty pants. Just don't go down into the grass. Last thing I need is you thinking one of the lawn ornaments is the real deal and start breaking stuff."

She chuckled. "Don't karate chop the garden gnomes. Got it."

Blade watched her walk out, unable to wipe the smile from his face.

"I can see how much you love her," his mom said.

Blade took a deep breath, and said the truth. "Yeah, Mom. I do." There was no other explanation for how gutted he'd been for the last six months without her. He'd known her for several months before, worked with her, became friends, and then lovers. It was the right order of things. The right order for the right woman.

Not that they were really together. He knew they weren't, but after that kiss last night, he'd decided to treat this time with Anna as the gift it was. He'd worry about what would be left of his mangled heart once this mission was over.

"Well look what the gator dragged in," a male voice he knew all too well boomed from the front door before he came into view.

Blade laughed. "Damn, Justin, when did you get so big?" he asked, stepping up to him and giving him a quick hug. He'd been his favorite cousin growing up, but they were also close in age.

"Wheaties for breakfast."

"Pfff, you need a good creole breakfast, yeah," his mom said, sliding into her accent.

"Where's Lauren?"

"He's right behind me. Wanted to drive his own truck 'cause he's got a hot date later."

"Stop talking about me, fuckers," Lauren said from the entryway, playful with an edge. That guy was always high-strung and moody as fuck. One minute he was a charmer and then next he'd have clouds in his eyes. But Blade figured everybody had their demons. Lord knew he did.

When he walked in, Blade's mom said, "Language, Laurent."

"Sorry, ma'am." He hugged her, and stepped over to shake Blade's hand.

"Where's your mom?"

"She's not coming."

"What?" his mom asked. "That cranky ol' hag."

"That's my mother you're talking about," Justin said, fighting a grin.

"And my whiny baby sister," his mom added with a shake of her head. "No matter. We'll chat and fill her in later."

Blade suppressed a groan. It might not be that easy. Aunt Barbara owned the equivalent shares of the estate as his mom did. Those in Blade's generation also received a share, but it was divided among their respective siblings. His father had tried to write Blade out of his portion and take controlling interest in the estate, but Blade knew he could fight it and win. He never did because it wasn't worth it to stir up trouble for his mom by pissing off his dad. Plus, he'd never done anything drastic to warrant Blade stepping in. After his dad passed, he'd gotten his rightful portion allotted to Bernadette's children, and since Brenna had died, the entire share went to him. Justin and Lauren had to split their portion. Even though all were all Beauregard grandchildren, Blade had the largest share of the three. But their mothers had more. There had to be a majority vote to implement changes, which meant they could overrule Barbara's stance if everyone here agreed. Otherwise, he'd need Barbara's support. And proposing to sell part of the land would definitely take some major convincing.

Even though he had no intention of actually selling.

"So why the sudden family meeting?" Justin asked. "Got any beer?"

"In the kitchen." His mom waved in that direction.

"I want to talk about the advantages of countering the Bartholomew Acquired Development offer to purchase some of our acreage."

Justin stopped walking away and faced him. The others froze.

"I know this go against my previous stance—"

"Everybody's stance," his mom said. "Why would you want to entertain it, sweetie?"

Blade sighed. He'd prepared this story, but just because it sounded good in theory to him didn't mean it'd be convincing enough for his family. "The area they're interested in is part of the higher plain of the property. If we sell them that, then we could go after the tract for sale south of our border. That area is more conducive for gators. I'm thinking, if we get the land to the south, we could build a lodge and take in more people during gator season. We're already booked years in advance for that time of year. We could command the same prices we do now but take on twice the amount of guests without sacrificing the area of land per hunter we advertise."

Lauren raised an eyebrow. "Hmm...not a completely

terrible idea. The only hunting shack on that end of the property is dilapidated because there's not enough wetlands up there for our guests to use anyway."

"Oh there used to be a producing swap up there, but the hatchlings died off years ago, and no new congregation formed. Just as well since it dried up," Justin said. "Doesn't matter. Mom would never go for selling *any* of the family land."

"Sweetheart, I don't know about this," his mom added, frowning.

"Look. I get it. I do. And I'm not even saying this is something we *should* do. I just think it's something we should seriously look into, rather than sticking to an outright *no* like normal. If after we look at everything and it seems like a bad idea, we'll walk away. No harm no foul. But if it seems like a great financial move for us, then we can sit down and decide if that's a step we want to take."

His mom's frown didn't leave, but she nodded slowly. "I guess there's no harm in analyzing it first."

"That's all I want to do at this point. I have no hope one way or the other how it turns out. Just want to dig into it."

"I don't have a problem with that," Lauren said.

"Mom might," Justin muttered.

"What about you, though?" Blade asked him.

Justin sighed. "What do you plan on looking into exactly?"

"Their offer and their financial records. See what their intention is with the land and if they're financially viable to fulfill their business plan...to start. Worst case, we can check out their methodology and maybe figure out a way to buy the land to the south without sacrificing any of our family land."

"It'll cost money to hire the right people to comb over that shit."

"Language," Mom muttered, glancing at Justin. Then she looked at Blade. "He's right. Professionals aren't cheap." His family was technically loaded. Plus, the business earned everyone a nice chunk of change every year. But the reason his family had money for generations was because they were frugal and their money was all tied up in trusts, which were separate entities in the eyes of the government. Everything was tracked, but it also kept their money separated from them individually. And that was good for both business and privacy.

"I happen to know an excellent CPA who focuses on forensic accounting and will help for free." He smiled at his mom.

She gasped.

"Who?" Lauren asked, eyes narrowing.

"Anna Sue?" his mom asked at the same time, but he could tell by the small smile forming on her face that she already knew the answer.

"And just who is Anna Sue?" Justin asked in a teasing tone his brother lacked.

"My fiancée."

———

ANNA STEPPED onto the grand porch and quickly pulled out her cellphone. Rick answered on the first ring.

"McMillian," he barked.

"Good afternoon, sir. It's Fisher." Whenever anyone on their team was on an op, they used burner phones. She had his contact information on her personal cell, but he was a stickler for following protocol.

"It's about damn time you checked in. What's the status?"

"Were you aware that Bayou Beasts isn't just an investment for Blade, but a family business with land that's been in said family for generations?"

Rick didn't respond right away, then said, "I was not aware of that. I do know the company is owned by several trust entities. I wonder if the SEC realizes this?" he asked, but she didn't get the feeling he was asking her, rather wondering out loud. It made her feel a little better knowing her boss hadn't kept information from her. "Any intel on Mason Showalter?"

"No, sir. We just got here today. His family is on their way now, so I hope to learn something once they get here or in the next few days when I'm given access to their books." And that was assuming the SEC's mark was even connected to Blade's business. At this point, that connection felt flimsy at best and farfetched at worse.

"Any news on Young?"

Oh, yes. He'd been arrested for murder. An arrest we have no flipping record of. But she didn't say any of that. She kept her mouth shut on that little tidbit, the reaction immediate and instinctual. That didn't mean she understood it. She was in law enforcement. It had been ingrained into her to divulge all details on a case, so why did she have the need to protect Blade's past from her boss? She hadn't hesitated in deciding to keep that information to herself. Deep down, she knew no matter what happened with this investigation, she wasn't going to risk Blade's freedom or his job. She'd follow her assignment as best she could, but she refused to sacrifice him to the federal gods of the U.S. government. She tried not to think too heavily on the meaning behind all of that.

Instead of the truth, she said, "No, sir. He's been polite, courteous, and helpful. Not even smoking cigarettes, which is odd since he was practically chain smoking on that op in Dallas."

"Keep an eye out and report anything you even think is suspicious."

"Yes, sir."

He ended the call, and without wasting any time, she immediately called Shelby since she wasn't sure when she'd get another chance to check in with her colleague.

"Hello?"

"Hey, girl, it's Anna. How's it going?"

Shelby chuckled. "You've been gone one day. I promise I'm not going to curl into the fetal position and cry until you return."

Anna laughed. "I know that. Just had a minute, so I thought I'd call."

"Well, the guys are all hanging around the garage looking at wedding magazines. It's the funniest thing I think I've ever seen."

"Oh God, you should take a pic and use it as blackmail later."

"Already done it. Twice."

Anna shook her head to keep from laughing again in an effort to stay focused. "So how's your mission coming?"

Shelby sighed. "I don't like this. These guys have helped the feds for years. I feel like we're betraying them."

"Shelby—"

"I'm sorry. I know I'm not supposed to get close to people on a case, and I don't want you think this means I'll always get close to people on other cases because I haven't been doing this for very long. This is just different."

"Believe me, I get it."

After a long silent pause, Shelby said, "Good. To answer your question, no, I haven't learned jack. I seriously don't think we'll get anything out of these guys until after the wedding. We should've booked this mission for two weeks later."

Anna agreed. No matter what the Bang Shift would've normally been doing right now, Brody's wedding to Xan had taken priority with all the guys.

As it should have been.

"So how's Blade?" she asked.

Such a loaded question. "He's fine. I mean, nothing new on my end." Why did she stare at her hand and the major bling on *that* finger?

"Mmm-hmm. You're forgetting about that night we had drinks with Viola about a month after the Dallas op. You muttered something about Blade and a mistake in between shots of tequila."

"I don't know what you're talking about," Anna said quickly.

"Sure," Shelby said slowly. "Just trying to let you know that if you need to talk about anything—off the record—I'm here for you."

"There's nothing to say." Because that was the only thing to say at this point. And probably ever.

"Okay, girl. I'll touch base with you if something changes."

"Is that your polite way of telling me not to check on you every day?" Anna smiled.

"Most definitely."

"All right. Message received."

They said their goodbyes, and Anna pocketed her phone, feeling productive having touched base with both Rick and Shelby in a short amount of time. Good thing, since Blade's family was probably here already, which meant she had to get her game face on and go back inside.

Yep, just needed to walk back in the house.

In a minute.

She took five.

And then it still took several minutes of breathing slowly to psych herself up to be the perfect girlfriend.

Fiancée. Jeez. She spent another couple of minutes staring at her ring. Not *her* ring, *the* ring. It wasn't hers.

When she was as ready as she was going to be, she walked through the French doors with her head held high as if she had every right to be there among his family.

"There she is," Blade said, grinning from ear to ear as if he counted down the seconds until she returned.

Anna smiled as she approached the small group.

"Damn, Blade, you didn't say she was hot." Though his words were playful, his gaze tracked her. She couldn't blame his family for being suspicious. It just showed how smart they were to question what was happening rather than blindly accept the cover story. She was glade she took those extra minutes outside to get her head into the game.

"Lauren," Blade's mother admonished.

Anna stuck her hand out to the guy who was closer, but she didn't do it for that reason alone. This man was the biggest in the room, and her training kicked in. Not that she felt threatened, but it was ingrained in her to suss out any dangerous ones first. "Anna Sue Fisher."

"Well, hello there, *cher*. Justin Beauregard."

"It's nice to meet you, Justin."

Blade grabbed her wrist and pulled her hand away from Justin. "Okay, okay, let her go." He chuckled and pointed at the other guy. "This is Justin's brother and my other cousin, Lauren."

"Actually it's Laurent, but I go by Lauren."

"Like the vampire?" Anna asked, smirking. The guy had dark, straight hair that swept over his eyes and an angular jaw. Slap some blood trickling from his lip and a trench coat, and he could totally pass as the fictional creature with an urban flare.

"But of course." He winked.

"Jesus, she's spoken for, you guys. Get your own girls."

"But we like yours," Justin said with an easy shrug.

"Not that anyone can miss that ring," Lauren said with a raised eyebrow.

Anna smiled at his charming cousins as she wrapped her arms around Blade. "Sorry, I only have eyes for one man, and that' never going to change."

Blade's mom giggled. "I'm so excited you're getting married."

"We are, too," she answered for Blade. Anna needed to show more excitement about it, instead of relying solely on Blade to sell the charade.

He kissed the top of her head. "I'm through with business for now. I want to take you on a tour of the property."

She gaped at him. "Like all of it?"

Justin guffawed.

"No, babe, not today. But over the next few days, I want to go over all of it. We'll ride wheelers over part, but I want to walk some areas tonight."

"I'll need to change my shoes."

He dipped and kissed her swiftly on the lips, then he swatted her on the butt. "Hop to it. We're burning daylight hours."

She ran up the stairs, changed into tennis shoes, and jogged back down. The shoes didn't really go with her outfit, but if he wanted to trek through swamps, she needed comfort over fashion. When she reached the bottom of the staircase, Blade was the only one standing there.

"Where's everyone at?"

"Mom's in the kitchen, looking at ideas for dinner. My cousins are leaving. They have other plans tonight but said they'd be back tomorrow for brunch."

"Oh, okay."

He took her hand, and they walked out the back door into the lush landscape of Louisiana.

"I can't get over how beautiful it is here. Back home there's nothing but cornfields as far as the eye can see." She chuckled.

"Kansas, right?" Did his thumb rub on the back of her hand?

"You remembered." They'd talked a lot in Dallas, but the more she looked back on her time with him, she realized she'd been the one doing most of the talking.

"Of course," he said softly. Yes, that was definitely his thumb tracing soothing circles.

"On that mission, I was the one with diarrhea of the mouth. I think it's your turn to spill your guts."

"That sounds gross on both counts." He chuckled. When she raised an eyebrow at him not backing down, he added, "Not much to tell."

"Well, since this one intersects with your personal life, I beg to differ. What if someone starts asking things I should know the answers to, or I say something totally off, like mention your favorite food but you're actually allergic to it."

He snickered. "You're an agent. I'm sure you're very good under pressure. In fact, I know you are."

"Brax," she breathed, just wanting him to open up. Not for the sake of her mission. She just wanted to know. Wanted him to let her in.

He didn't say anything as they walked, but he held her hand tighter. When they reached a beautiful weeping willow next to some marshy land, he stopped and gazed at it. "This was my sister's favorite tree."

Oh God. When she wanted him to open up to her, she hadn't expected he'd broach something so personal. She'd quickly figured out his sister was gone when his mom had shown her the family photographs. But that had been initiated by his mother, not him. Now, Anna held her breath as the sliver of light came through the door he was opening for her, letting her *in*. She had wanted to ask about the girl before, but now she didn't dare utter a word. After several seconds where it felt as if Blade was going to crush her hand, he finally spoke.

"She was killed." His grip eased, but she refused to pull her hand away and shake feeling back into her fingers, afraid of breaking the spell. "She was found beaten and stabbed. Autopsy showed she'd also been raped." He made a sound of disgust. "Or at least had rough sex prior to the murder."

Her heart hurt for him, but that didn't stop her investigative instinct from kicking in. "They catch him?"

"No."

"Any semen?"

"No."

"Have a boyfriend?"

"A douchebag."

"Was he cleared?"

Blade's gaze slid to her. His eyes hard, challenging. "He disappeared."

Holy shit. *Holy fucking shit.* She didn't have to ask what happened because she knew from the look in his eyes that he was the one who'd made the guy vanish.

She was stunned in silence.

If she posed the question, he'd either outright lie about it, or he'd confess. *I don't want to hear either one.* A lie would throw up walls. A confession would leave her no choice but to arrest him. Everything prior to this point was circumstantial and easier to ignore. Jesus, her heart pounded so hard as she contemplated what to say.

Finally, Anna gave a slow nod and looked over the water. "Just as well," she said smoothly because she didn't know how else to respond. Anything else was too dangerous. Maybe after she'd had time to mull over everything, she'd ask, but not right now. Right now, she couldn't think of anything beyond what he admitted using very few words.

He disappeared.

"Fuck," Blade breathed, yanking his hand away and stalking over to his left before turning and going to the edge of the water.

The air around her suddenly felt very thin and fragile, so Anna decided not to follow him. Instead, she walked straight ahead to the water directly in front of the tree. The grass was taller in front of her, much higher compared to where Blade stood off to the side. She really couldn't see where the water started, so she didn't get too close. No way did she want to risk falling into swampy waters.

She stood there looking over the marshy area, glancing over at Blade every few minutes and wondering if he was going to blow. Even from this distance, she could tell he was practically vibrating with emotion. The man was either about to spew everything and damn the consequences, or he was forcing everything behind that door and locking it shut with a great amount of effort. Either way—

The grass suddenly moved, and a horror much greater than hearing details of a murder confession crashed into

Anna a second before she screamed. Stumbling away from the bank, she only got a few feet from the edge before she tripped over a root, her palms slamming on the ground behind her as she fell.

"Anna!" Blade rushed over just as an alligator emerged through the weeds. She barely caught Blade whipping his shirt off, the material flying on top of the animal and covering its eyes. Without hesitation, Blade grabbed her as she came to her feet and dragged her back, jogging away as he sheathed a scary looking knife—a knife she hadn't seen him holding until that moment—and pulled out a 9mm handgun.

The alligator thrashed, dislodging the shirt, and turned back the way it came rather than coming after them.

"I didn't know you were carrying," she muttered, instantly missing her firearm as the adrenaline began to wane and she started to shiver.

He turned toward her as he shoved his gun in into his jeans, and then he clutched her arms. "Jesus, Anna, you do *not* go near the water."

"Why didn't you just shoot it?" she heard herself ask, but she wondered if the words even all came out of her mouth.

He ran a hand through his hair as if he was trying to calm down. If so, the storm in his eyes told her he was losing that battle. "There's only a small area on the head you can penetrate that'll actually kill a gator. I didn't want to piss it off, or risk you getting hit from a ricochet."

She balked. "What would a knife have done then?"

"Fuck, you're bleeding." He grabbed her wrist and stared at her hand. He growled something and tugged her into the house, obviously done hearing her adrenaline infused rambling.

Because a freaking alligator almost had her for dinner.

Holy shit. A shiver rocked through her, setting off a stream of constant tremors as Blade guided her through the darkened halls. Even her teeth betrayed her when they began to chatter. She was a skilled FBI agent, for crying out loud. She has come face-to-face with some of the country's most dangerous criminals without breaking a sweat.

Hell, without breaking a fingernail.

But there was huge difference between gators and gangsters.

"Are you even fucking listening me?"

Was he talking? Anna couldn't get her jittery brain to make her mouth fess up that she hadn't heard a word he'd said.

Great. She'd made a rookie mistake regarding danger, and now she was having a meltdown.

In front of the man who owned a part of her.

A part she knew, even in the state she was embarrassingly in, she'd never get back.

If she had her wits about her, she'd be looking for a hole to crawl into right about now. Preferably one that was alligator free.

"Jesus, you're shaking."

But when he wrapped her in an embrace, the tremors eased slightly and she melted into his warmth, pretending she'd always have a place right there in his protective arms.

CHAPTER SEVEN

Blade did his best not to yank Anna through the halls of the house as he fought off the knot of irritation that settled deep within his core. She could've been killed. Fucking attacked at the very least. Even lost some limbs.

"Don't you know how precious your life is?" he muttered to her. "You should always, *always* be on guard to make sure nothing happens to you. Jesus Christ, Anna, you work in law enforcement. Doesn't that require some sixth sense shit when it comes to dangerous things? Do you think it gets any more dangerous than wild animals?" he yelled.

He wasn't being fair. He knew that. But he was still in fight or flight mode, and since he wasn't fleeing, that left only one option. Being a dick.

"Are you even fucking listening to me?" he asked, flipping on the light switch of the bathroom as they walked in. He didn't look at her while grabbing gauze and peroxide because he needed a few more seconds to rein in his misplaced anger. Because through the furious haze, he knew whose fault this really was.

His.

Blade knew the dangers of the swamps. Hell, his company devoted time to safety, requiring hunters to view videos on the dangers of the sport prior to hunting on their land. Anna wasn't a hunter. She'd never lived in Louisiana or an area where alligators lurked. The worst thing in the wild she'd probably faced before today was a crow that'd gotten loose in the cornfields. Yeah, this was all his damn fault, and he was taking it out on her.

With a deep breath, he deposited the medical supplies on the counter and faced her. If any irritation was left, it evaporated in an instant when he saw how pale she was.

"Babe?" He clutched her upper arms, worried she might pass out. "Jesus, you're shaking." He pulled her to him, wrapping his arms around her tightly.

"N-no. I d-did hear what you said." She shivered, and he rubbed slow circles on her back.

"Forget it. I was just freaking out."

Her little laugh was laced with nervous tension. "Makes t-two of us."

"Anna," he breathed into her hair. "I'm sorry. I won't let that happen again." He couldn't control the animals, but he could control how close she got to danger. And he damn well would.

"I-I'm getting b-blood on you," she said, and she tried to pull away from him, but he wasn't having it. He squeezed her, not letting her budge.

"Don't care."

As he held her, the trembling slowed. It could've been ten seconds or ten minutes, he didn't know. Time ceased to process. When she sighed and snuggled into his chest with the last of the tremors, he kissed the top of her head.

"Better?"

She nodded and shifted, which he reluctantly allowed

because he seriously didn't want her to leave the security of his arms. No harm could come to her if he just held her forever.

With a little freedom, she didn't step away, though. Rather, she looked up at him, color back in her cheeks, her big eyes trained on his. God, she was so beautiful. How she made him feel, it almost hurt to look at her. Feelings he'd long suppressed. He gazed for as long as he could, but to stop the almost suffering, he dropped his forehead to hers, cutting off his view of her, because it was times like this that made it too painful to look at the one thing he wanted most and couldn't have.

"Thank you."

"Nothing to be thankful for." That wasn't entirely true because he was damn well thankful for her. Though, he knew what she meant with her appreciation, and she didn't need to be thankful for him rescuing her from the alligator when he was the one to put her in that danger in the first place. "It was my fault."

"Blade," she breathed, and leaned back to look at him.

Those eyes. He could get lost in them, start saying things that were best kept buried deep. Yet, as he continued to gaze at her, the urge to confess his feelings was too much to bear. Without conscious thought, his mouth opened.

Anna's tongue peeked out, wetting her lips.

Blade groaned and leaned down, not even pretending to resist. He was sure when his mouth opened, he was going to spill feelings welling inside, but now he had zero intention of talking.

He was going to kiss her. There was no stopping him. But he refused to crash his lips to hers and take her like a rutting animal, especially when she was just recovering from another beastly encounter. She deserved tender, to be treated as if she was some rare fragile glass. Because she was precious to him.

Priceless.

And incredibly fragile.

His mouth grazed hers, and the soft sound she made almost destroyed his will to go slow. A will she apparently intended to break as she pushed her tongue into his mouth and grabbed his head, demanding him with her actions just what she really wanted. Jesus, he was trying to take his time, but any desire to worship her slowly exploded into the mindless frenzy he'd been trying to keep at bay.

Blade lifted her and turned, crushing her into the door as he took her mouth the way she needed. The way his body wanted.

Anna wrapped her legs around his waist, perfectly aligning his aching cock with her core, her tongue diving into his mouth, dueling with his, and he didn't even give a fuck if she won that battle.

Because, fuck, the way she tasted, he wanted nothing but to devour her.

When she gripped his hair, Blade ripped his mouth away to pepper kisses along her neck.

"God, you feel so good," she breathed.

He only grunted in response because to say anything else would require his mouth leaving her body, and no way in hell was that happening. He continued his path downward to her chest, yanking her shirt out of the way as he reached her breast. She gasped when his mouth landed on her nipple, and he wasn't sure if it was the sounds coming out of her or the sudden taste of her flesh—or both—but in that moment, fire raced up his spine, igniting him, fueling him to take her, have her. Nothing would stop him from making her his over and over. He didn't give a damn if that alligator got into this room and he'd have the chance to avenge her almost attack, he still wouldn't stop. Absolutely nothing would stop him.

"Getting blood on you," she panted.

Fuuuck. Okay, maybe that. Not that he cared about the blood on his clothes. He'd throw them away for all he cared. But he needed to make sure she was fine, and the cut wasn't too deep.

Groaning, he pulled back and grabbed her wrist to inspect it.

"Doesn't look too bad." He deserved a metal for getting out a complete sentence.

She tugged her hand away and stepped over to the faucet. He cleared his throat as he rummaged around the cabinet for bandages. Her hand was mainly scraped, but there was one cut that needed doctoring.

"You got a towel you don't mind getting bloody?" she asked, and turned off the water.

"Here." He grasped her wrist again and patted her palm dry with gauze. After he was pleased no more moisture remained, he quickly added some ointment and a bandage to the worst cut.

He rubbed her fingers as he kept his gaze trained on her hand. He had to admit he loved the sight of that ring on her finger. He liked it a whole hell of a lot more than he should. Just because he loved her didn't mean things could be any different for them when they were through with this mission. After shaking that thought away, he still didn't look away. Her battle wound treated and no longer an issue, he knew if he glanced up at her face, he'd be a goner anyway, no matter what tomorrow brought them.

"You're shaking," he heard himself say.

"Different reason this time."

His gaze shot to hers. "Anna."

"Don't make me beg," she said softly.

A surprised laugh escaped him. Not the most romantic gesture to make, but he couldn't help it. She was so damn adorable.

"Never," he breathed before planting his mouth onto hers again.

Blade briefly fisted her hair, but he knew he needed to get her to a bed before he fucked her right here in this bathroom.

Not that he was terribly opposed to the idea.

Releasing her locks, he grabbed her rear-end instead and lifted her. Anna wrapped her legs around his waist as he fumbled with the door. He knew this house inside and out, a fact he was incredibly thankful for right now as he walked her blindly to his room.

She made a sound of protest when he dropped her beside the bed and then gasped when he suddenly whipped off her shirt.

"Impatient?" she breathed with a light chuckle.

"Been way too long, Anna."

"Mm-hmm." She reached for his belt, but he gently blocked her progress. If she touched his cock right now, she'd get a real taste of just how impatient he was. Even though he wanted to take her fast and hard, he needed to take his time and worship her slowly.

Or as slowly as he could manage...*after* getting her clothes off. He had zero patience when it came to divesting her of the fabric barrier between them, and accomplished that feat in record time. She reached for his shirt, but he picked her up and laid her on the bed.

"Brax," she whispered as he forged a path of hot kisses down her body. God, he really loved it when she called him by his name. He muttered her name in response, but once he said it, he couldn't stop himself from repeating it between all the gentle kisses he placed on her as he made his way down her toned body. Why didn't roses smell this good on the stems? It was as if once it touched her skin, it created this bouquet so much sweeter. And Jesus, her skin was just so soft. Up until Anna, Blade had usually gone for curvy women. There had just been something about that particular type that made him feel manly.

But knowing Anna could knock him off his feet and draw her gun before he could blink was an entirely different rush. The muscles flexing before him now could be lethal, and the fact that she was wiggling and moaning below him...that he could bring this strong, independent woman to this state was sexy as hell. And that was beside the fact that he actually loved this woman.

God, but he loved her.

When he reached the apex of her thighs, he grabbed her knees and pushed them as far apart as he could. Anna gasped at how quickly he managed to get her legs open. His gaze snapped to hers as he brought his mouth down to her core, but as soon as his tongue touched her, her eyes squeezed shut, her head rolled back, and she let out the hottest fucking sound he'd ever heard.

He licked her like he was starving, avoiding her clit, and it didn't take long for her to get antsy. But as soon as she lifted her hips, silently begging with her body, Blade gripped her waist and held her still as he continued his sensual assault.

Her groan of protest morphed into one of pure ecstasy, and his needy dick ground against the bed, seeking relief. He couldn't wait to be inside her, but he was loving having his mouth on her too much to stop right this second, and he really wanted to push her over the edge before he pushed himself inside her.

So he continued to torment and tease her, licking and sucking, giving attention to every part of her exposed to him except the one little nub she so desperately needed touched.

"Please, please, please," she began to chant when she got to the point she couldn't take it anymore, the force of her squirming almost bucking him off her with each word she uttered.

Feeling like she was right on the precipice now, Blade shoved two fingers inside her and finally flicked his tongue over her clit. Her pussy clamped down on him right before she let out a scream, and he continued to lick the same spot as he finger-fucked her through her orgasm. He was so absorbed he hadn't realized she'd grabbed his head at some point, holding him to her a she road out the high, and holy fuck, that was hot as hell.

The moment her grip lessened, Blade rose up, shucked his clothes, rolled on a condom, and thrust inside her.

"Oh, Jesus," she said, and grabbed his shoulders.

With her body still gripping his dick, he'd pray to anybody she wanted because she felt like pure heaven. He pushed into her over and over, trying not to be too rough, but damn if he didn't want to just take her like a man possessed. He hadn't had sex since the last time they were together, and it was too easy for him to get lost in the sensation and not be tender.

"You okay?" he asked, hoping he was being careful enough.

"I'm not gonna break." Then she grabbed his ass and forced him to take her harder.

He laugh-groaned at his tough little hellion and the

sexual gauntlet she threw down. A challenge he was all too ready to accept.

He grabbed her hands, held them above her head, and fucked her with renewed purpose.

"That what you want?" he asked, and swooped down to pull a nipple into his mouth.

"Yes!" she screamed as he sucked on her, switching from one breast to the other.

God, he'd missed how expressive she was. But it also turned him on so much that he knew he wouldn't able to last as long as he wanted. Because, fuck, he wished he could go for hours before losing it.

"Oh, you're gonna make me come," she said through a pant, and squeezed his hands harder as she thrust toward him.

He plowed into her, kissing his way up to her ear. "Come on, baby," he breathed, and as if she was waiting for permission, she flew, her body bowing up yet clamping down at the same time as she let go and came all over his cock. His own body couldn't wait for any verbal go ahead from her as fire lit up his spine. He followed her over, fucking her with shallow thrusts as he let out a groan of release, not slowing until he was spent.

Perfection.

She was utter perfection, and he couldn't wait to have her again and again and again.

He bit back a moan when he pulled out. After quickly taking care of the condom, he pulled a yawning Anna into his arms and held her. They still had to meet his mom for dinner, but they had time for a quick nap. Besides, he really didn't want to let go of her just yet.

As she fell asleep in his arms, he couldn't help but feel

the love pouring out of him...and a ghost of concern over their conversation in the meadow before the gator attacked.

Because even though he didn't come right out and say it, he all but confessed he'd murdered his sister's ex. Not that he was worried about his past actions—he'd kill that sonofabitch all over again if given the chance—he was concerned how Anna would treat him once she had time to adjust to the news.

She'd either accept him no questions asked.

Or she'd arrest him.

As he drifted off, the last thought he had was both of those possible outcomes were terrifying for completely different reasons.

———

ANNA ROLLED over and stretched her deliciously sore muscles. After Blade had made love to her, she'd fallen asleep in his arms, and it had felt so right. She'd been dead to the world when he'd woken her up to get ready for dinner. Then she'd been frazzled getting ready, followed by being so focused on playing her part at dinner that Anna hadn't thought about what had happened in the meadow.

And she wasn't thinking about the alligator freaking her out either.

She wasn't sure if Blade had given it any thought. If she had to guess, she'd think not, because after they'd gotten back to his room following dinner, he'd had a one-track mind...and that track led to the bed.

He had bent her over the edge of it and had taken her from behind, only shoving clothes just enough out of the way to achieve penetration.

Then, Blade had guided her to the bathroom where they'd showered together.

And had sex against the tiled wall. She'd later realized he'd planned it since he'd brought a condom with him into the shower.

That had been totally fine with her.

After they gotten out, dried off, and snuggled into the bed, he'd stripped her bare and pushed into her gently, taking her almost painfully slowly until they'd come together what seemed like hours later. By the time they'd finished, she'd been too exhausted to even think straight, much less stand up, which meant he'd had to help her walk to the bathroom to get cleaned again. Anna couldn't remember the last time she'd had sex four times in one day and her poor vagina was not happy with her right now.

But aside from her sated lady bits, there was something more pressing causing her discomfort. The realization that Blade practically confessed to murder.

What was she supposed to do with that information? She knew what she was *supposed* to do. Her professional instinct was screaming at her to call her boss and tell him what she knew.

Her heart was yelling just as loudly, though.

And her brain was trying to decide which one was more important.

I mean, he didn't say he killed that guy. Blade had told her he'd disappeared. Any number of things could have happened to him.

But what also bothered her was that she wouldn't blame Blade if he *had* done anything. There was a right and a wrong to everything, but she understood the human nature to protect. Hell, she'd made her career out of safeguarding people in one fashion or another.

Annnd now I'm justifying murder. Jesus, she needed to take a step back and look at this objectively, she thought as she rolled out of bed. Blade was already awake and downstairs with his mom, waiting on his aunt to arrive for brunch. Anna was in no rush to join them. She needed time to process things, so she grabbed a change of clothes and made her way to the bathroom to shower.

She scrubbed herself clean as her mind jumped from thoughts of murder and sex, both acts of passion stemming from polar opposite extremes. It was no wonder she felt flustered.

By the time her skin glowed red, Anna decided she needed more info directly from the source before she decided anything. She didn't even want to think about confiding her suspicions in him with anyone else, and waiting until she knew more details would buy her time before she had to make that kind of judgement call.

She dressed in a skirt and a blouse, conservative like yesterday. This time, she wasn't taking any chances, though, and strapped her piece to her leg. If any gators came after her, she'd be prepared to shoot. She just hoped she hit the spot that'd kill it. She smirked to herself. Of course, she'd be able to hit the target. She was second in her marksmanship class.

Taking deep breath, she gathered the last of her resolve and made her way to where Blade's family had surely all congregated by now. As she descended the stairs, the voices grew, so she followed the sounds of laughter and ribbing.

"...Then he ran it in for a touchdown, yeah. Broken ankle and all."

"It wasn't broken, Lauren."

"Oh please, Justin. Your foot was damn near dangling."

"It was still a hell of a game." Anna would recognize that voice anywhere.

"And a shitty few months after. I had to push you around in that damn wheelchair all over the place."

"Language," Blade's mother said.

"Dude, I remember you taped racing stripes and stuck flags onto that thing." Justin laughed.

"I forgot all about that. Y'all stayed here because your house wasn't wheelchair accessible," Blade said.

"Reminiscing about your youth?" she asked as she walked into the room.

"Good morning, sleepyhead," Blade said as he made his way toward her. He kissed her forehead.

"Beauty sleep and all that."

"*Cher*, with your natural beauty, you could pull all-nighters the rest of your life," Lauren said and winked at her.

"Not natural. It's NARS." She smiled at him and focused her attention where she needed it. The coffee pot.

"Must be a girl thing," Justin said with a frown. She didn't expect these men to know about makeup brands.

"It's a girl thing," she said, using his words and turning her back to the guys as she fixed her cup of morning ambrosia.

"You must be the lovely Anna Sue," a lady said. Anna turned around, but the reply died on her tongue. This was Blade's aunt? Justin and Lauren's mother? Wow, Blade's family had really great genes.

"Anna, this is my sister, Barbara." Not that Anna needed the clarification from Blade's mom, who also looked too young to have a grown son.

"Jeez, I bet you still get carded for alcohol," Anna finally breathed.

Barbara laughed delicately. "If they know what's good for them."

Bernadette had called her sister an old hag. *Must be a sibling rivalry thing.* "Well, you're just as pretty as Mrs. Young—Bernadette," she quickly corrected before Blade's mom could do it for her.

"Prettier," Barbara said with an unapologetic smile. Bernadette rolled her eyes.

Yep, sibling rivalry, if only good-natured competition.

"So why are we eating here and not Boudreau's?" Barbara glanced at Anna. "They have the best shrimp and grits."

"I told you, Mom, Blade wanted to talk about the business," Justin said.

"Yes, well, that was my polite way of getting the conversation going." She looked at her sister. "At least tell me you have mimosas. One can never have too much Vitamin C."

"Or too much champagne," Bernadette muttered before stepping out of the room. Before she could return with the ingredients for the popular brunch beverage, Blade quickly explained his proposal to his Aunt Barbara, who had the same number of shares in the company as his mom. Getting her on board with the idea would save them a lot of trouble of out-voting her.

"So you see, I think it makes sense to entertain the purchase offer. Checking it out doesn't lock us into anything."

"Except we'd be selling family land," Barbara said, shaking her head.

"True, yeah," Lauren said. "But if we sell that section of land, we could invest in more gator hunting property. It could be very profitable."

"And you do love money, Mother," Justin said.

"It's not the money. It's the principle."

"Since when did you start making decisions based on ethics?" Bernadette asked as she mixed drinks.

"What's that supposed to mean?" Barbara snapped.

"She just means business decisions shouldn't be emotional," Justin said.

"And that's another reason I want Anna to look at the books. She doesn't have a horse in the race, and she's damn good at numbers."

"Doesn't have a horse in the race?" Barbara scoffed. "That huge ring on her left hand says otherwise." She glanced at Anna. "No offense, dear."

"None taken. What I think Brax meant to say was that I'm not emotionally invested in this place." She stepped toward him and rubbed his arm. "At least not yet. I'd be leery of selling something that's been in his family for generations. I certainly wouldn't advise it unless it was a smart decision all around."

He bent down and kissed her forehead. "If anything, her findings could help justify an increase in our land value. Put us in a better position to get a loan against the property to increase income other ways."

"That's true. If I can determine they should offer more and up their offer, the market value increases."

Barbara sipped her mimosa before saying, "I guess there's no harm in looking. It's not as if you can make a decision without the rest of the family."

Blade's lip twitched, but it was apparent he quickly suppressed the smile he was about to show. "Great. I'll run into town this afternoon and talk with their realtor. Let him know we wanna look at the books to determine the viability of their offer. Tomorrow, I'll pull our financial statements for Anna. She can start going through everything."

"And how long do you think this will take?"

"Hard to say," Anna said.

"We have to go back soon for a wedding, but if we get electronic copies of the information, we can take it with us."

"Yeah, it doesn't take long to read reports, but I like taking my time when I analyze fiscal data."

Barbara sighed. "Fine. Just keep me updated." She looked at Bernadette. "How soon until we eat? I didn't eat dinner last night."

Bernadette chuckled. "Out with that fine man again?"

"A lady doesn't kiss and tell."

"For the love of God, please don't," Lauren said.

"C'mon, let's go into the dining room."

"You did good," Blade murmured to Anna as the followed the group to the feast spread.

"You too." She smiled at him. "This looks great," she said to his mom.

"Wish I could take credit for it. We have full-time cooks."

Blade pulled her chair out for her, but she barely noticed. Her gaze was locked on what looked like cream cheese and berry stuffed French toast. She might have even groaned. When he chuckled beside her, she figured it was likely.

Light conversation carried on around her, and she did her best to add to it when possible, but for the most part, she was too occupied with devouring her decadent meal. Soon the conversation died down while delicious food was consumed and tipsy beverages flowed. Blade only drank coffee, deciding to skip on the mimosas. Come to think of it, she hadn't seen him drink since she'd been back. Not that he drank much before, but he had done so occasionally. Anna had a mimosa, but Bernadette made them strong, so when she finished her drink, she switched back to coffee. When they finished with brunch, they walked into the great room and said their goodbyes. Lauren seemed antsy to get back to the woman he'd taken home last night, which of course, Blade and Justin ragged him about a little, all in good nature. Barbara pushed him about meeting her, and Lauren couldn't seem to hide the smile this woman gave him, saying if things keep going like this, she'd be introduced soon. Right after he left, the others quickly followed. All the while Anna played the perfect little fiancée, all smiles and charm. The sugar rush she just inhaled helped.

"That went well," his mom said once their guests left.

"Yeah. I need to run into town. Mind showing Anna the sights this afternoon while I'm gone?"

Anna's gaze shot to Blade, but he focused on his mother. What the hell was he doing? He should know they were partners, which meant she'd be going with him. If he went without her, she could miss vital information. And why would he want to go out without her? What the hell was he up to?

"Of course, dear."

"I don't want to put you out," Anna said quickly.

"Oh, it'll be fine. We can talk weddings. Men don't like dealing with all the details."

"Great." Blade kissed his mom on the cheek and her on the lips. "I shouldn't be gone more than a few hours, babe."

She narrowed her gaze at him, but he pretended not to notice. Oh yeah, he was definitely up to something.

After he walked out, Anna's mind raced. She needed to figure out a way to follow him. Their time here had suddenly been cut short because his mother had the foresight to get everyone together. Anna wasn't going to have many opportunities to dig into Blade and his life.

"I have a friend who owns a dress shop. Give me an hour to get changed and we can run out to the city."

No way in hell was she trying on wedding dresses, but this was the opening she needed. "That works. I'm going to do some sightseeing while you're getting ready."

Bernadette frowned. "I can show you around."

"Oh, I'd love for you to show me all the cool things. I was just going to drive around to kill the time. It's so beautiful out here."

She nodded slowly. "Okay. I shouldn't be more than an hour. Would you like to take my car?" A motorcycle started outside, signaling she didn't have much time to get out there before Blade drove off. "Sounds like Blade's taking the bike."

Even better. "Then I'll take Brax's." Anna quickly grabbed her purse and keys and rushed outside. She saw him head down the driveway, so she bolted to the vehicle and followed. She knew she was acting suspiciously, but hopefully Bernadette wouldn't think anything of it.

Letting her FBI training kick in, Anna stayed far enough behind Blade that he wouldn't notice her. Thankfully, the road was winding enough and there were a few cars spaced out between them that it made it easy for her to stay hidden. On the straightaways, she allowed a couple more cars between them to help camouflage her. Thank God Blade didn't speed because no way would she be able to weave in and out of the little traffic and stay incognito.

Once they reached town, Blade pulled up to a large building beside a strip mall that housed several businesses. As she got closer, she pulled into the parking lot of a restaurant on the opposite side of the street, but parked facing the building Blade parked in front of. He got off his bike and glanced around as if he was looking for anything out of place before he turned his attention to the front door.

What the...

Surely he wasn't going into that large building. Oh, but he was. Anna watched silently as Blade walked into what looked like the law office of Ward and Associates.

And just why the hell was he going to see a lawyer? On a Sunday. She couldn't ask him, so she did the only thing she could. She pulled out her phone and called a member of her team.

"Childers," he answered.

"Carson. I need you to pull data on a law firm for me. Ward and Associates."

"Well, hello to you, too. Oh, I'm fine. You know, same ol', same ol'."

Anna rolled her eyes. "Hi."

"Now was that so hard?" He chuckled. "So what's this about?" he asked, all business.

She paused, quickly thinking how much she wanted to share at this point. She hated lying, so she'd be vague instead. "Not sure yet. It's a name that's come up. Could be nothing." And that was the truth. "I want this to stay between us, at least until I figure out if it's relevant."

"Go against protocol?" He tsked, but with obvious humor. "You got it."

Oh the irony. She didn't have it. Lately, it felt as if she didn't have a handle on anything at all.

Besides, Anna had a sinking feeling that whatever Carson found on the firm would only complicate things more.

She glanced at the clock as she ended the call. She hadn't killed enough time to avoid the whole wedding dress fiasco. Anna groaned and backed out of the parking lot, heading back to Blade's property.

To try on wedding dresses for a pretend wedding to the man she loved for real.

Fuck, complicated indeed.

CHAPTER EIGHT

BLADE KNEW he was in deep shit.

Ever since the afternoon he bolted and left Anna Sue home with his mother, she'd been distant with him, and he had a feeling it had nothing to do with his mother's impromptu bridal session. Although, he'd love to have been a fly on the wall watching how uncomfortable she got trying on dresses, but he had a feeling that would've just added to her irritation with him.

He wasn't sure if it was something he did or said or if maybe Anna had reached her fill of lying to his family. He'd stayed by her side most of the time, trying to make it easier. The only time he left was when he went into town to talk to his sometimes lawyer about past transactions the development company looking into buying his family land had already completed, hoping to find clues based on the areas they were focusing on.

And he hadn't taken her for a very specific reason. His past.

Colton Cormier wasn't just a real estate lawyer. He'd

also been a close friend of Blade's growing up. He, along with Mason Showalter, ran around with Blade and his cousins all the time. Colton played football with Justin, but also loved video games like Lauren. All four of them loved to hunt and fish. Blade and Colton had confided in each other a lot over those early years, and there was a time Blade trusted him with just about everything. The one thing he'd never told Colton was what really happened to Jeremiah. Hinting at it with Anna was the closest he'd ever gotten to telling anyone.

When Colton decided to go to law school, Blade was relieved he'd never confided in him about that night. And then when Colton went to work for Jeremiah's father, Fletcher Ward, he was even more grateful he never spilled the beans. Not that he blamed the guy for going to work for that man. Mr. Ward had the largest practice in several surrounding parishes and employed a lot of associates and partners, specializing in just about every area of the law. It wasn't as if there were many other professional options for Colton outside of private practice, which he'd just end up competing against the powerhouse firm. Honestly, Blade didn't expect Colton and Mr. Ward to have any relationship beyond a cordial, professional one. Hell, the old man probably didn't even know Colton's name, but it would be stupid of Blade not to expect the worst. They lost touch over the years, so there was no way for Blade to know how much time Colton spent around Mr. Ward, a powerfully persuasive man. Unless he felt confident that Colton's loyalty hadn't shifted, Blade didn't want to bring him around Anna. For all he knew, Colton had started believing Mr. Ward's version of events...which were much closer to the truth than Blade's. He needed the guy's real estate expertise, but he didn't have to bridge that gap between his past and his present to get it. Anna was too fucking smart for her own good. A fact he'd normally be very prideful of, but it was too dangerous of a trait where his past was concerned. Once he sussed him out and analyzed whatever information Colton had, he could then introduce Anna to him—if necessary—and bring her up to speed.

Not that the trip produced much intel. BAD was buying up land all over the place, without what seemed rhyme or reason. Plus, the company itself had been created through several trusts, so it'd take time to dig into the actual people behind it. He and Anna spent the next several days gathering financial documentation, meeting with BAD's own real estate lawyers and company liaisons—low level paper pushers on the company food chain—to go over everything. That time together had been about the only time the two of them spent in each other's company. Anna hadn't ventured out with him when he spent the afternoons trekking over the rest of the estate. Not that she was really free to go along. His mother kept her busy with wedding preparations, probably fueling her anger toward him even more and more with each passing day. No matter how early he tried to turn in each night, she was already in bed. By the time they'd left late Thursday, staying not quite a week, and with Anna practically throwing his grandmother's ring at him as soon as they got in the car—he was sure he had a place on her shit list.

"You're getting oil all over the floor," Brody said matter-of-factly, and Blade cussed, yanking the nozzle back. They'd gotten back really late last night, and he knew with everything going on with the wedding, the guys were behind at the shop. Rather than sleeping in like he'd wanted, Blade dragged his ass out of bed and came in.

It wasn't as if he had a luscious, warm female body

cuddled up next to him. Oh no, Anna hadn't even let him help her carry her bags into the FBI safe house when they'd returned. Shelby had come out all sleepy-eyed and assisted, which meant Blade couldn't even try to talk to Anna without raising her teammate's suspicion. All attempts in the car on the way back had quickly been shot down. She'd donned earbuds and scanned documents on the ride back. He was worried he'd ruined his chances with her, but he was bound and determined to clear the air. He just needed to get her alone and away from the excuses of work.

He glanced to the side and watched as Anna's colleague, Shelby, bent over the hood with a crescent wrench. She was a beautiful woman, that was for sure, but she didn't hold a candle to Anna. From what the guys said, the girl knew her shit when it came to cars. He'd bet his right foot that Anna had never changed oil herself. Or a tire. He almost laughed at the recent memory...something he could do now after spending half the morning chewing Roc out for taking his jack. He'd taken some of his frustration out on Roc because he hadn't been able to do it with Anna yet. He knew it wasn't fair to his coworker, but all he had to do was remember Anna walking those few miles with her bum ankle, and any caring for Roc's feelings fled.

"Want to know why this car can't go over sixty-eight?" Roc asked no one in particular.

"Because at sixty-nine, that bitch flips over and blows a rod," Shelby replied without missing a beat.

Yeah, she apparently not only had the skills of a mechanic but the mouth of one, too.

Brody snickered.

Hunter guffawed.

Bear growled something about sexual harassment.

"Aw, c'mon. It's just a joke," Roc defended.

"Dude, my brother used to tell jokes like these all time when he was a teen. Used to make my dad so mad."

"He still a mechanic? Work keeps up like this, we might need to hire some help," Bear said. Blade figured he was only partly serious. If they ever extended their workforce, the guy would have to be as comfortable with a gun as he was a torque wrench.

"Nope. Went into the military after high school. Though he's been talking about retiring soon. Not sure if he'd leave the corn fields of Nebraska for the rice fields of Arkansas."

"Screw your brother, you should leave the feds and join us. You'll make a hell of a lot more money," Roc said.

"Just because I'm in Arkansas doesn't mean I'm screwing my brother, hotshot," Shelby said as she continued working.

Blade cracked a smile for the first time since getting back. Hell, probably one of few times in the last six months. It felt good to get lost in work. Really, it felt good being near Anna again. Even if she was probably pissed at him about the whole wedding dress shopping thing.

The door chimed, and he took his focus off Shelby and glanced at the door, meaning to only look briefly before cleaning up the mess he'd made, but when he saw it was Anna and she was already staring right at him, he couldn't take his gaze off her. He started to move toward her, but he noticed the smile she had plastered on her face looked forced. Maybe now wasn't a good time.

Roxie walked in right behind her, and without even looking, he could sense Bear stiffening. Yeah, the two of them had a history. How much, no one was sure. Not that anybody asked, nor did the two of them volunteer. After shit hit the fan that night at the old train depot, Blade briefly wondered if they'd move passed whatever was keeping them apart. After all, Bear had held her, comforted her, and had chewed everybody a new asshole who'd come within ten feet of her that night. She'd not only been kidnapped, but she'd been taken and held against her will by her own cousin. A man who'd also been Bear's best friend not that long ago. But whatever truce they'd called, it had been temporary. The two of them had avoided each other like the plague ever since.

"Oh, sweetie, you're getting grease under your nails," Roxie said as she made her way to Shelby, not even looking in Bear's direction.

"I ran into Roxie at the gas station," Anna said, shoulders still tense.

"Yeah, and I told her we need to have a girls' night. So that means, you need to finish up what you're doin' here and come with us. Xan's gonna pick us up in a couple of hours, and you need to be ready."

Shelby glanced up from under the hood of the 1970 El Camino she was working on. "That sounds like it involves alcohol. Can't drink while on the job."

"You won't be on the job once you clock out," Roxie said.

"Not as if you're working a case," Brody said. "Besides, my future wife can't drink." He smiled, but it slowly went away. Yeah, that man was still getting used to the idea of being a new daddy.

"She's the designated driver," Roxie said. "The rest of us are getting shit-faced."

"You've been working hard here. You deserve a break,"

Anna said, but Blade could tell her response felt forced. What the hell was wrong with her? Anna wasn't much of a partier and probably wasn't looking forward to going out, but that didn't seem like it would bother her that much. She must really be pissed at him.

He took a step toward her, but she lifted her hand, effectively stopping him.

Looking toward Shelby, she said, "Finish up what you're doing and let's go. I think after this week, we all need some drinks." Her gaze cut to Blade, but didn't stay long enough for him to motion her to the side to talk.

"Oh, I should call Heather and see if she wants to come," Roxie said.

"Y'all driving into Little Rock?" Roc asked at the mention of Heather.

"Hell no," Hunter said. "My sister has finals."

"Then I'll call Maya," Roxie said.

Hunter narrowed his gaze, knowing he wouldn't say his girlfriend couldn't go out with the girls. That was a sure-fire way to get his balls kicked...and by his girlfriend.

"We'll let them study," Xan finally said. "But we're still going."

Roxie laughed. Shelby wiped her hands off as she stood. Anna looked around, avoiding eye contact.

"We're going to have so much fun tonight!" Roxie exclaimed as the ladies made their way to the door. "It's going to pull double duty as the bachelorette party."

"This is going to be a long night," Brody said, frowning.

Yeah, Blade agreed. Completely.

———

IT WAS STUPID. Anna knew it was freaking ridiculous, but she was a woman and could admit chicks as a collective group did not always land on the reasonable side of things. And as she glanced sideways at Shelby, Anna was fully aware she'd taken a trip to Crazyville.

Because it did not escape her attention that Blade had been checking out her colleague when she'd arrived at the shop this afternoon. Shelby was a beautiful woman, one who did not act as if she completely believed that, which Anna figured made her more attractive to the opposite sex. Shelby confidently working under the hood of that antique car, completely absorbed in her task, oblivious to the men in the room gaping at her, was serious single-woman goals. Being appreciated and admired for one's skills and not just one's body.

Though she'd recognized the look every man in that shop had sported. Attraction. Oh, Anna didn't think any one of them would really act on it. Hell, Brody was getting married in a matter of days, but even he'd been awed by Shelby's handiwork.

At least this was what Anna kept reminding herself every time she drifted back to the memory of Blade eyeing Shelby. She hoped as the night went on and the drinks started flowing with the girls that the flashback would happen less and less. Because deep down—like most women —she knew she was acting silly about the whole thing. When she'd stopped at the gas station, she'd been on her way to the shop. There'd been enough distance between the two of them, and she felt it was time to clear the air. Plus, she still had a job to do. Not that Blade had given anything away while they'd been together, nor had she found anything suspicious in the company paperwork. She wasn't sure how much longer they'd get to stay on this assignment, and she needed to get in as much time as she could with him. For work, of course.

At least that was what she told herself.

Until she walked up and saw him watching Shelby through the windows before she even reached the door.

"I'm ordering a round of shots!" Xan said as she waved at the waiter who'd been by twice already. The first time, Xan said they needed to work on their drinking game plan before ordering. The second time, they'd all ordered margaritas. Anna and Roxie got theirs on the rocks, Xan and Shelby frozen. Of course, Xan's was alcohol free.

"Girl, you don't want us to be able to get outta bed in the morning, do ya?" Roxie asked with a chuckle.

"Well, ladies, can I get y'all something else?" the waiter —who barely looked old enough to be serving alcohol in the first place—asked when he slid up to their table. "Your drinks are almost ready."

"Apparently, the bride-to-be wants us to get lit," Shelby said with a wry smile.

"A round of tequila shots for my gals," Xan said to the waiter, and then to the girls, "I mean, tequila goes with margaritas."

"That it does," Anna said.

"Oh, jeez, you don't have to explain the virtues of shots," Roxie said, and gave Xan's hand a squeeze. She turned to the waiter. "Can you bring them out with our margaritas? Make sure hers is a virgin."

"Been a long time since I was linked to virginity." Xan smirked.

"You got it." He winked at Roxie and left the table.

"Oh, did you see that?" Shelby asked, her gaze following

the guy's retreating back, leaving no question as to what she was referring.

"Pfft," Roxie said, waving off the comment. "He's practically Chad's age," she said, referring to her teenage son.

"And yet, he's not," Shelby said.

"Eww, close enough," Xan said. She also had a son Chad's age. In fact, from what Anna saw, the two guys seemed to be inseparable...even hanging together with their girlfriends.

"Gotta agree with Shelby on this," Anna said. "There's a big difference between a high school boy and a twenty-four-year-old man."

"Really?" Roxie asked. "What's that?"

"Stamina?" Anna asked, deadpan.

Xan busted out laughing, and the other girls followed.

"That's totally a thing," Anna said, defending her answer.

"Oh, looks like I just missed something good," the waiter said when he appeared at their table with a tray of their drinks.

Roxie snorted. Shelby elbowed her and faced the dude placing their drinks in front of them. "Just girls being girls."

"I like girls being girls."

Anna wasn't even going to comment on that. She grabbed her drink and took two big gulps.

"Can we get some cheese dip?" Xan asked. "If I can't have liquor, I should at least get to eat carbs."

"We can get whatever you want," Roxie replied, and then downed her shot. "And an order of wings," she said to the waiter.

The next round of drinks came out first, and Xan pouted when she was the only one not given a shot glass.

"How's the morning sickness?" Anna asked before downing her shot.

"It's awful. I forgot how bad it can be." Xan frowned, eyes glossing over as if she was lost in thought. Anna figured she was probably remembering the first time she was pregnant. Xan had been married to a mob boss who'd abused her. She'd gotten away from him and was now living her happily ever after with Brody. It gave Anna hope that maybe things do work out in the end.

At least for some people.

"How's the wedding planning coming?" Anna asked to pull Xan back into the present.

Roxie groaned. "She's a bridezilla."

Xan gasped. "I am not! I just want everything the way I want it. And I want it to happen before I get as big as a house."

"I was wrong. She worse than a bridezilla. She's a *pregnant* bridezilla." Everyone laughed except for Xan. She feigned being offended before cracking a smile.

"At least your shotgun wedding is gonna be beautiful," Roxie said. "Roc's barn is going to look so good."

"I still can't believe he let you use it," Shelby said. "He's a bit of a—"

"Asshole," Roxie said, finishing her statement. "Yes, yes, he is."

"He's not that bad," Xan defended. "I mean, you definitely don't want to cross him, but he has his sweet moments."

"Might want to check with Heather on that," Roxie muttered.

"What's that supposed to mean?" Anna asked. She'd heard comments here and there about Hunter's sister, Heather, and Roc.

"He was there when she was rescued, and it seems he's a bit smitten," Xan said.

"Well, that's an understatement," Roxie said, rolling her eyes.

"I thought he wasn't seeing anybody," Shelby said.

"They're not together," Xan said. "Heather is young, and Roc is—"

"Determined," Roxie said with a raised eyebrow. "That man is freaking determined to have her."

"Must be nice, having a guy who would stop at nothing to show you how much he wants you," Anna said, thoughts drifting to Blade.

"Yeah, no shit," Roxie said with an edge in her tone.

"Speaking of Bear," Xan said, and took a sip of her virgin beverage.

"Nobody said his name," Roxie said.

"You going to the wedding with him?" Xan continued as if she hadn't said anything.

"He didn't ask."

"You could bring it up."

"Um, no. If he wanted to go with me, he'd have said something. So he doesn't. He doesn't want a damn thing to do with me." She shifted in her seat, a smile forming on her face. "Besides, I'm the maid of honor. I'll be busy keeping you from becoming a runaway bride. I mean, someone has to make sure this thing goes off without a hitch."

"Except for the two getting hitched," Shelby said and hiccupped. "Oh, sorry."

"Jeez, you haven't had that much to drink," Anna said.

"Been too busy working cases to drink."

"Yeah, but you're not working a case now." Roxie raised her glass and toasted with Shelby. That was the second time her colleague had referenced being on assignment. Anna would have to talk to her about watching what she said in the future. It was true that they were working on a case, but no one here knew that. The fellow agent needed to be careful how she worded things. The guys on the Bang Shift were very sharp and could easily pick up on Shelby's word choice. She had no doubt these women were equally as smart if not smarter.

"What about you?" she asked Anna. "You going to the wedding with Blade?"

"Oooh, nice question," Roxie said, leaning in toward the group as if she was about to hear some big juicy secret.

"Um, no. Why would I?"

"You know you're invited, right?" Xan asked. "I mean, even if Blade is too dumb to ask you himself. I want you there." She looked at Shelby and said, "The both of you."

"Technically, I was already invited," Shelby said cryptically and grabbed her drink.

Anna felt the blood drain from her face. Was that why Blade was staring at her when Anna arrived at the shop earlier today? Because he'd asked her coworker to go with him to the wedding?

"What? Spill!" Xan said.

Shelby's gaze darted to Anna. Jesus, she was going to be sick. Then Shelby glanced at Roxie before looking at Xan. "Doesn't matter. I turned him down."

"Aww, you have to tell," Roxie said.

Shelby shifted uncomfortably in her seat. "Nope. It was an innocent offer, but I didn't want to cause any waves." Then, below her breath, she muttered, "I don't do that to my team members."

"Innocent," Anna scoffed. Blade was many things, innocent wasn't one of them. Her little admission felt much heavier than the words themselves.

"Huh?" Shelby asked, frowning.

"Nothing," Anna said, waving her off before picking up her drink. It wasn't Shelby's fault she was naturally beautiful and men couldn't help but want her. Apparently, Blade wasn't immune either.

"Since this is my pseudo bachelorette party, I think we need to play some games."

"Sorry, girl, we're saving games for the baby shower. Tonight is all about saying goodbye to the single life," Roxie said.

"Shouldn't there be strippers for this?" Shelby asked.

Roxie smirked.

"Oh, no, I can't have strippers," Xan said.

Right then a couple of guys walked into the private room they were boozing it up in.

"You didn't," Xan said.

"Oh, I so did," Roxie said, raising her hands right when the music cranked in the room. "Woo-hoo!"

The guys started bumping and grinding to what sounded like the soundtrack to one of the *Magic Mike* movies. They danced around the girls, and each time they got near Xan, she shooed them away like they were a couple of flies, but would giggle each time. She was having fun, and that was the important thing.

"You can't keep them at bay forever," Anna said, smiling.

"Oh yes, I—eek." The dark-headed dude scooped up Xan and carried her over to a chair in a clear area of a makeshift stage. She giggled, but before they could even get down and dirty, the door slammed to the area they were in.

Anna glanced to the side, thinking one of the employees had closed them off to keep other patrons from witnessing the debauchery, but she caught long blond hair zipping by her as Brody walked up to where his future wife was sitting. The man looked like a freight train barreling toward the entertainment. On instinct, Anna got up. It was her job to protect and serve, and she had a feeling one—if not both—of these men was about to meet his maker.

Someone grabbed her shoulder, and she whirled around, hand on the person's wrist, ready to rip it off, flip him around, and shove his hand behind his back.

"Whoa, whoa," Blade said, grabbing her hand and waist to keep her from the defensive move she was about the put on him.

"What the hell are y'all doing here?" she yelled over the music.

Rather than answer her, he turned her around, and to her great amusement, she watched as Brody did an exaggerated striptease. Well, without actually taking his clothes off. He shook his ass and lifted his shirt up a little as he danced around a laughing Xan.

"Oh." Anna looked over her shoulder and smiled up at Blade.

"Hi." He'd said it so softly, she could barely hear him, but the gentle greeting was sweet nonetheless.

"Hey," she said back to him. Maybe it was the alcohol, but she couldn't remember him ever smelling so good.

Heat flared in his eyes and, without another word, he took her hand and guided her outside.

Anna turned to him when they reached the alley, but he didn't give her a chance to speak. Before she could open her mouth, he pushed her against the wall, slipping his hand behind her head so she didn't bang it against the brick, and slammed his mouth over hers.

She moaned, but any sounds she made were swallowed by him as he devoured her. God, he tasted almost as good as he smelled. When he forged a path of hot, wet kisses along her neck, Anna sucked some much needed air into her starving lungs. "Brax," she breathed.

He groaned against her skin and thrust his jeans-covered cock against her at the sound of his name. Jesus, she loved getting that kind of reaction from him.

It didn't escape her that she was irritated with him earlier, or that she'd been avoiding him, but her body didn't seem to care. At. All. She needed him, and no matter what, she was going to get what she wanted.

Him.

All him.

He tugged her spaghetti strap down, his mouth following the path his hand cleared. She groaned when he sucked in her nipple, and it either fueled him further or wasn't enough because his other hand yanked her skirt up. Anna gasped when his hand dove into her panties, and she instinctively hiked her leg up around his hip, trying to get closer. They were out in public. This was so wrong on so many levels, but it only made it all the hotter.

"Fuck, you're so wet."

She couldn't form a coherent sentence if she tried. Instead, she fumbled with his belt, not wanting to wait another minute to have him inside of her.

Blade leaned back, and faster than she could register, he dug out a condom, sheathed himself, and lifted her up.

"You ready for me?" Although he'd asked, he thankfully didn't wait for a response. Blade pushed into her, and she held on tightly as he pounded her into the wall. Gone was the care he'd shown her head. Anna was sure there'd be scratches on her back.

She didn't give a flying rat's ass.

"Touch yourself," he breathed.

What? No way. She shook her head and thrust her hips against him. He leaned back a little, pushing into her at a slightly different angle, hitting all the right places.

"Oh, God."

"Do it, Anna."

He slowed his movement, which infuriated her because she was so close already, but she wouldn't be able to get off at this pace.

"Please, baby. I want to see you touch yourself." He leaned closer to her, his mouth at her ear. "I'll give it to you good if you show me."

Jesus, this man was lethal. Of its own volition, her hand skimmed down her body and slipped into her panties.

"Fuck, yeah," he said as he watched, his hips increasing in speed the closer she got. He groaned and fucked her like a madman. Anna had been so close already that when she slipped her finger between her legs, coupled with the intensity of Blade's thrusts, she hurdled into orgasmic bliss. She might have screamed, but Blade's mouth descended onto hers the moment she fell over that precipice.

His movements became erratic and, moments later, he groaned into her mouth, stifling his own sounds of ecstasy.

They held each other as he slowed, the harsh kiss turning tender, soft. When he pulled away, he kissed a few more times before letting her land on her feet. It took her a moment to get her wits about her, during which time Blade took care of the condom and fastened his pants. He helped her set her own clothes to rights.

"Come home with me." It wasn't a question. He probably was too scared of what answer she'd give him if he posed it as one.

"Yes," she said. Because there really wasn't any other

option anyway. She'd missed him. Everything else aside, she missed him.

He smiled at her. Kissed her nose once, twice, and smiled at her again. "Let's go."

He took her hand and pulled her behind him.

"What about everyone else?"

"They can find their own way back."

Who was she to argue?

THE LAST TWENTY-FOUR hours had been crazy-ass busy. The morning after the bar incident, the garage had closed for the day and all of the guys had been out at Roc's putting the finishing touches on the barn. Around mid-afternoon Blade had thought for sure they wouldn't get finished, but the guys pushed on. Shortly after three o'clock, Xan, Roxie, Heather, Maya, and Anna had shown up to decorate. The guys were still working on one of the walls, but since they were all working against the clock, the ladies started on the other end. Right as the men finished the last project, the women had worked their way to that end. It had been almost perfect timing.

The colors Xan had chosen were an array of purples. Not just one shade of the violet hue, but many. She even used lavender in some of the table arrangements. The colors and smell reminded him so much of his sister, but for the first time since she'd died, he welcomed her favorite color and scent. He still missed her terribly, but up until now, the reminder of her life would just throw him into memories of her death. It was an ugly cycle that never allowed him to reminisce about the good parts her of short time on this earth.

Last night, he hadn't wanted to leave Anna's side, but best man duties called. Brody had stayed at Blade's place last night, and Anna had stayed with Xan. He was pretty sure Roxie had stayed over with the girls well into the night. If she ever went home at all. He'd left Brody to his slumber this morning, having left as soon as he got dressed. Blade wanted to be at the barn for last minute deliveries and to be present when the vendors arrived. He figured it was his job to do all the final stressing for the man of the hour. It wasn't as if the man let him throw him a bachelor party. The few times he brought it up, Brody got almost violent in his refusal. Just as well. They were too balls-to-the-wall busy anyway.

He adjusted a few table arrangements that had gotten knocked over, spread out the sheer curtain things—the ladies had called them something, but he couldn't remember the term—and signed for the food. He'd even had some gator meat delivered as a surprise for the happy couple. Gauge showed up with the liquor, and Blade helped him set up.

"You guys done yet?" Roc asked as he walked into the large open space of the main barn.

Blade whistled low. "Looking sharp, man. Who you trying to impress?" he asked Roc. Although everyone knew the answer to that.

"Don't think Hunter will let you dance with his sister," Gauge said.

"Fuck you. And you," he said to Blade second.

"Not even if your hair was longer," Blade said. "Have you heard from the photographer?"

"Yeah, she called twenty minutes ago. Got lost. Should be here any minute."

Blade checked the clock on his phone. "Shouldn't Roxie be here by now?"

"I am here," she called out as she pulled a mobile crate behind her. Blade jogged over to meet her and took the plastic bin from her load.

"What is all that?" Roc asked when she opened the first box by the liquor table.

"Last minute decorations." She pulled out photos in various frames of the happy couple. "Help me pick out some places to put them." She pushed one of the champagne bottles over and it caught on the wood, almost tipping over. Roc grabbed it before it could spill.

"Don't get shit on my galvanized sheets."

"Bet you say that to all the gals," Roxie said, and winked at him.

Gauge chuckled. "You're good."

"And all the guys do say that to me." She wagged her eyebrows and dug into the box for another photo. "Where's your date?" she asked him.

"Don't have one."

"Don't tell me you couldn't find a girl to come with you."

"The one I asked said no."

Roxie gasped and smiled. Blade didn't understand the exchange, but he had more important things to focus on. He grabbed another picture frame from the box, and just as he walked off, he heard Roxie say, "I'm sure Heather would dance with you if you asked." Followed by a growl from Roc.

After putting a nice image of his best friend and his future wife on the table where they'd be eating, he caught Anna walking in, and he froze. Goddamn but she looked beautiful. Short cream-colored skirt, button-up blouse with the few top buttons undone, shiny new cowboy boots. She was rocking this country-western themed wedding like nobody's business.

"I need some ginger ale," she said as she walked toward him.

"Oh shit, Xan sick?"

"Well, she's growing a baby inside of her. Damn sure not something I wanna catch." She smiled.

Blade chuckled. "Good thing this wasn't a sunrise wedding," he said as he walked over to the drink station. He'd already thought to get non-caffeinated beverages for her and figured it wouldn't hurt to keep something around to soothe nausea. He dug it out of the cooler and handed it to Anna.

"This ceremony wouldn't happen if she had to get up before the sun did. Thanks." She gave him a quick kiss before darting away with the drink. The reaction had happened so quickly that Blade wondered if Anna even thought about it first or just kissed him out of instinct. He was okay with whatever that answer was.

"Why is Anna practically running out of here with a soda?" Brody asked.

"Hey, when did you get here? Ready to say goodbye to the bachelor life?" Blade clapped him on the shoulder.

"Answer the question." Brody shoved his hands into his light-colored slacks.

"Xan's just a little quea—oh no you don't." Blade grabbed Brody's arm as soon as he tried to retreat. "She's fine. You will piss her off something awful if you see her before the wedding. If she needs help, Anna will let us know."

Brody looked at the door where Anna Sue had disappeared, obviously contemplating going after her.

"C'mon, man. Don't make me fail completely at the gig."

He pulled out his phone, but Blade grabbed it from him. "I'll call Anna." He pocketed Brody's phone, retrieved his own, and hit Anna's name in his contacts. As soon as she answered, he asked, "How's the bride?"

"I thought we covered this. We're not really getting married."

Blade laughed at her quick wit, but he'd be lying to himself if he thought he was okay with never making her his in every sense of the word. "I mean the one getting married today. The groom is about five seconds away from storming in there."

"No! She's fine. The bad feeling has already passed. Yay, ginger ale! Now keep him away, Brax. I'm serious." She ended the call and he smiled to himself. He hoped he'd never get used to hearing her call him that.

"She's fine. If you try to go in there, I'mma have to take this knife out of my pocket and wrestle you to the floor."

Brody narrowed his gaze at him, but attitude Blade could deal with. He seriously didn't want to take on the Neanderthal...because Brody would straight up kick his ass and leave him mangled on the ground.

The next thirty minutes flew by in a flurry of final touches, and before Blade knew it, he was standing at the front of the altar next to Brody. He watched as Scott walked his mom down the aisle, but he couldn't go more than a couple of minutes without looking at Anna. Hell, he couldn't even say if the ceremony was beautiful because there was only one person who held his attention. When Anna lifted her hand and tucked her hair behind her ear, he couldn't help but notice just how bare her finger was. He'd been glad she hadn't tried to give his grandmother's ring back to him before they got into the car because it wasn't as if he could have left it at his ranch. He'd put it in the safe at his house, but deep down he knew there was only one place it belonged.

"I know pronounce you man and wife. You may kiss your bride."

Cheers jerked Blade out of his reverie, but he felt a pang of sadness at those words. Not because he wasn't happy for his friend. He was extremely grateful Brody had found happiness. No, it was because he hadn't realized just how much he longed to hear those words himself.

He'd never planned on getting married. Ever. And he'd been okay with that. Until now.

As Blade watched the happy couple descend the stage and walk along the petal-laden path, he knew whatever he'd felt about marriage before had forever been changed. And that made everything worse.

Because Anna would never marry him, and even if she would, he'd never allow the woman he loved to give up her career in law enforcement just to live her life with a murderer.

———

"SO, who's that woman with Bear?" Shelby asked Anna as she scooped out punch and began filling the plastic cups. Brody and Xan had already cut the cake, posed for photos, had their first dance, and were making their rounds while everyone else danced now. Bear and Bachelorette Number Three were currently tearing up the dance floor.

Anna had seen him walk in with that leggy redhead and

had immediately looked for Roxie. Not to see her reaction. Oh no, Anna wanted to make sure the feisty little chick wasn't about to go ratchet on his date's ass.

"I have no idea."

"Maybe she's someone from the city?"

"Who knows. Probably fixed her car or something."

"Gave her a lube job?" Shelby said, and winked.

"You gotta stop with the dirty mechanic jokes."

"Why? The men at my family's shop would be proud. No matter how much my dad tried to shield me from that, I still grew up around filthy jokes." She shrugged. "Different era."

"No doubt."

"Blade looks hot," Shelby said with a crooked smile. Anna's hackles rose. She hadn't forgotten about Shelby being asked to the wedding by him. She'd wanted to ask Blade why he'd asked her. She'd ultimately chickened out, thinking he'd had to come because he was in the wedding party and probably assumed Anna wouldn't come with him. But that was just a guess.

"What's that supposed to mean?"

Shelby lifted her hands up in a placating gesture. "Just that you're a lucky woman. That's all."

"How did he ask you anyway?" Because she was a glutton for punishment.

"What do you mean?"

"You can stop playing coy, Shelby. I know it was Blade that asked you to the wedding."

Shelby gaped at her. Then busted out laughing.

"Dude, it was *not* Blade."

Anna frowned at her. "You said something about not agreeing because of your teammate. If you didn't mean

Blade who asked—*oh*," Anna said, realizing the truth. "Gauge."

"Yep. I know Viola is married, and their relationship—if any—was a long time ago, but you still don't go out with guys your friends have been with. Girl code." Shelby put her hands on her hips. "I can't believe you'd think I wouldn't tell you if Blade asked me out!"

Anna sighed. "Sorry. You were working at the shop that day and you mentioned teammate...what was I supposed to think?" Anna waved off that question. "Never mind. Doesn't matter. I'm sorry. You're totally right."

"Good. Now put the ladle down because your boyfriend will be over here in three—two—one—"

"He's not my boyfriend," Anna whispered heatedly.

"Hello, ladies," Blade said. "Can I have this dance?" he asked, taking Anna's hand into his right as a slow song started.

She nodded and he escorted her out onto the dance floor. Blade held her tightly as they swayed to the music, and Anna couldn't help but wish they could freeze this moment in time.

"You look beautiful, by the way. I haven't had a chance to tell you that."

"Thank you. Xan said dressy casual, and the wedding was in a barn. I figured that meant cowboy boots were in order."

"In the south, we call them shit kickers."

Anna leaned back to stare into his eyes. "Just how far north do you think *Kansas* is?"

His eyes danced with humor. "Damn yankee."

"Redneck."

Blade's head fell back as he laughed out loud, and Anna

couldn't help but join in. When the humor died down, Blade asked, "You like the gator?"

"Um, is that a euphemism?" She winked.

"Damn straight." He clutched her tighter and kissed her forehead. She liked this playful side of him.

"Tasted like chicken."

He scoffed. "That's sacrilege."

"Not if you love chicken." She smiled.

He shook his head, but his lips quirked.

All too soon, the song ended, and Blade leaned down to kiss her cheek. "Thank you."

"My pleasure," she said right before the DJ announced the next song. It was a fast song that was apparently popular because several of the women rushed to the floor. As she tried to leave, Xan ran by and grabbed her arm.

"Where do you think you're going?"

Anna stumbled behind her back to the center of the floor.

"I love this country shit!" Xan yelled, and started doing some dance that apparently everyone knew. Several people chuckled like there was more meaning behind her words, but Anna just tried to follow along. She was never into the club scene, but she could spot a line dance a mile away.

Cameras flashed. Champagne flowed. And Anna kept stealing glances at Blade whenever she could as the day turned into night. Christmas lights repurposed lit the barn, casting a warm glow that rivaled the stars. It was truly a beautiful night.

Brody whisked Xan away before it got too late, either wanting some alone time with his bride, or wanting his pregnant wife to get some rest. Either way, they'd stayed a lot longer than Anna had figured they would. Soon after, some of the guests left, and no matter how well Roxie hid her jealously, Anna still caught her looking after Bear as they left the party. Seeing how happy Xan was with her new husband, and how unhappy Roxie was that her love was with someone else, made Anna want to reach out and hold onto Blade for as long as she could. She watched the two extremes tonight, and if she had her choice, she knew which one she'd pick.

Once the party started winding down and all that remained were the Bang Shift guys—Bear had returned after taking his date home—Roxie, Anna, and Shelby, started helping Roc clean up. It took hours, and by the time the last candle was extinguished and napkin recycled, Anna was practically dead on her bare feet. She'd long ago lost track of her boots.

"C'mon, babe," Blade murmured right before he wrapped his arm around her, her shoes in his other hand. Anna let him guide her to his SUV, belt her in, and when the pulled up to his place, she hadn't even been quick enough to unhook the seatbelt on her own. Blade scooped her up and carried her into the house. She'd expected him to take her to bed, so she was a little surprised when he put her down in the bathroom. She looked at him, but he silently began pulling the bobby pins from her hair. Once he was done with that, he turned on the shower, undressed her and himself, and nudged her in. He washed her hair, scrubbed her body, and took care to rub her back a little as he did so. He was so tender with her, she had to fight tears. Why couldn't she just tell him what was going on? Why did she have to lie to him about what she was really doing here? She wanted nothing more than to come clean emotionally just as she was coming clean physically.

When the water started to run cold, he quickly washed himself, turned off the faucet, and dried them. Neither of them bothered with the pretense of any nightclothes. He eased her onto the bed and spent what felt like hours worshiping her body. She'd and Brax had had sex a few times now, but this was different. For the first time in her life, she was made love to.

She would forget about the pain this reality would cause for now, and just be with him. Be with him like she wanted. Like she wished she could forever.

CHAPTER TEN

WHAT IS THAT NOISE? Anna groaned when the insistent sound wouldn't stop and rolled over to try to distance herself from it. It took her about two seconds to realize there was something big and warm right beside her and she snuggled into Blade for about half a second. Then she realized what that sound was. Cussing softly, she gently rolled back over, grabbed her phone, and accepted the call before she left the room to silence the ringer.

"Hello?" she whispered as she walked down the hall, hoping Blade hadn't been disturbed enough to wake up fully.

"Good morning, sunshine!" Carson said. "Know what day it is?"

"I don't even know what hour it is." She glanced at her smart watch. "Just past dark-thirty. Why are you calling so early?" They'd only been in bed a few hours. Jesus, her feet still hurt from those new cowboy boots.

"It's the twenty-fifth. I figured with all the festivities yesterday, it'd slip your mind."

Oh crap, it totally had. She knew the date was coming

up, but as soon as she and Blade returned to town, the wedding preparations had taken precedence over everything.

"We don't know when Mason Showalter will be making his monthly call. I need you to be on the ready."

"I will be." Although spying on Blade was the last thing she wanted to do. "Any word on Ward and Associates?" She'd asked Blade that afternoon where he'd gone, but he'd given her some story about errands and left it at that. He was hiding something from her, and she didn't like it. She'd been irritated with him for days after that. And yes, she knew it was a double standard. She was hiding something from him, too. The real reason she was working with him.

"Yeah, and you're not gonna like it. Shit is suspicious as hell."

"What do you mean?"

"Well, Ward and Associates looks to be a large law firm. Like one of the top three largest in the state. There's tons of info on all the partners and associates. Not that it helps much because everyone knows everybody from small towns anyway. But the last living founding partner, Fletcher Ward, has a lot of bad luck...or extremely good luck, depending on your perspective. The other three founding partners died earlier in their careers, leaving Ward with controlling interest in the firm. Want to tell me what I'm looking for specifically?"

No way was she telling him Blade had gone into that law firm. She didn't want his name attached just yet. "Just a company that showed up in the paperwork"

"Mmm-hmm," he said like he didn't believe her for a second. "Well, looks like Mr. Ward also had a son. Found birth certificate and death certificate. Cause of death for one

Jeremiah Ward is listed as *in absentia*, but no specifics were identified."

"Missing," she breathed, dread filling her as she remembered verbatim what Blade had told her in Louisiana...about his sister.

"She was killed." His grip eased, but she refused to pull her hand away and shake feeling back into her fingers, afraid of breaking the spell. "She was found beaten and stabbed. Autopsy showed she'd also been raped." He made a sound of disgust. "Or at least had rough sex prior to the murder."

Her heart hurt for him, but that didn't stop her investigative instinct from kicking in. "They catch him?"

"No."

"Any semen?"

"No."

"Have a boyfriend?"

"A douchebag."

"Was he cleared?"

Blade's gaze slid to her. His eyes hard, challenging. "He disappeared."

"Yep, but it looks like Ward pulled the right kind of strings to get the death certificate issued prior to the regular waiting period. All signs point to him being a powerful man. So powerful in fact that he has many companies. One that's very important to our investigation. Bartholomew Acquired Development."

"Wait, what?"

"Why does that surprise you? You just said Ward and Associates was on the paperwork."

Fuck! "Not on the offer paperwork." Which was true.

"Oh. Well then you stumbled upon the law firm of the man who apparently also owns the company trying to buy Blade's family land. That or it was great investigative work."

"Thank you."

"Rick thought so, too."

Double fuck! "You already told him," she said quickly, not posing it as a question.

"Yes, and I think you should tell me why you sound panicked."

No way. If she told him she happened across the law firm because she watched Blade walk into that building, he'd think Blade was behind the land purchase. Hell, she'd think it at first, too. Until she logically thought about it and realized that Blade already owned his family land. Of course, Carson could make the argument that maybe Blade wanted controlling interest or a part all to himself. No, she didn't need anybody on her team looking into any connection between Blade and Mr. Ward, and not because of the land offer. If her theory was right, the link he did have was the one he didn't want exposed, ever. Anna would be willing to bet her career on the fact that the murder Blade had been arrested for was for Jeremiah Ward's disappearance. Not that it explained why Blade went to that law firm on a Sunday afternoon.

"Not panicked. I just thought you were going to tell me whatever you found first."

"You were busy playing fake fiancée and planning a wedding."

Anna shut her eyes. She knew it was her responsibility to report everything she'd learned, but she still needed time to get some answers. It was on the tip of her tongue to ask Carson to look into Blade's sister's death, but if she did, he'd be quick to make the same connection Anna had regarding Jeremiah Ward. "I was doing my job," was all she said. Although, she'd have to admit, she was doing a crappy one at that.

"I don't like the way you sound," Carson said softly. "Wanna tell me what's going on?"

"Nope. I just need to dig further." That was true.

"Well, we're trying to find Mr. Ward to do some prying ourselves, but we've been told he's on vacation right now."

"Hopefully, he'll return soon then." And hopefully, he was really out of town and not at the very bottom of a shallow grave.

"Maybe the call today will shed some light on what's going on."

She doubted it. Mason Showalter was the least of her worries.

———

BLADE TURNED the last of the bacon over in the pan, browning it to perfection before removing it. "Breakfast is ready," he called out.

"I don't think it counts as breakfast at three o'clock in the afternoon," Anna said coming up behind, giving his waist a gentle squeeze, and swiping a sizzling piece for herself.

"Hey, that's stealing," he teased.

"I need to feed my appetite," she said with a wink. He chuckled and scooped a pile of eggs onto a plate for her.

"Good thing I have just what you need." She smiled, but it didn't reach her eyes. Blade wasn't sure if it was lingering exhaustion from yesterday or what, but she seemed a little distant today once they'd finally gotten out of bed.

He placed her plate in front of her and took a bit of his own eggs when his phone rang. He glanced at the caller ID and suppressed a curse. He didn't want to deal with business stuff right now, but Mason was a stickler for schedules. His old friend had moved off a long time ago, and they'd lost touch over the years. Once Blade got to the point he needed help with his financial planning, he'd reached out to Mason. He talked to him once a month about the investments he handled for him.

"Sorry, babe, I gotta take this."

She perked up slightly, but nodded before picking up another piece of bacon.

"Hello?"

"Hi, stranger. Long time, no talk."

"Um, one month to be exact."

Mason chuckled. "Well, one month since we talked about your financial holdings. But I think you'd be interested to know I received a phone call from Colton the other day."

Blade glanced at Anna out of instinct, but she was busy eating her meal. "He didn't say he was going to call you."

"He found out something interesting about Bartholomew Acquired Development, and needed some unbiased advice."

Blade didn't like the sound of that. "I'm listening."

"Colton did some digging into the company and found one of the members belonging to one of the many trusts that made up the company is Fletcher Ward."

Fuck. Blade schooled his expression. He knew that Mr. Ward was a very rich man and hand his dirty little hands in many capital ventures, but this revelation threw a huge fucking monkey wrench into Anna's operation. If Fletcher Ward was part owner of Bartholomew Acquired Development, the company who'd been trying to buy his family land, then that made things all kinds of fucked up. Fucked up because Blade knew Mr. Ward would have ulterior motives in purchasing that land. Very powerful reasons. And they all related to the fact that Mr. Ward never hid his suspicions that Blade was behind the *disappearance* of his son. When charges didn't stick, Jeremiah's father tried whatever he could to hurt Blade. It was his mission in life to ruin him one way or another, and swooping in and taking his family land was one way to do just that. Fuck! Truth was, Jeremiah had been out to the land many times before Brenna died. Without an actual body, any DNA found could be explained away, but Mr. Ward probably assumed there was evidence to be found that would definitively link Blade to what happened.

No way in hell was Blade giving that man a chance to find clues. Not that there were any. He made sure of it.

The gators made double for sure of that.

But he needed to stop this operation right fucking now. He couldn't even pretend to let his family entertain the offer presented by Ward's company.

"I take it you understand the gravity of what I just said."

"Yes," Blade said smoothly.

Mason sighed. "You don't have to say anything. You never did. As far as I'm concerned, that fucking little bitch got what he deserved. Whatever it was. But the last thing you need is Fletcher Ward and his cronies on your ass."

"Agreed."

When Blade didn't elaborate, Mason finally asked, "Is somebody with you? Your new fiancée, perhaps?"

Shit. Blade had to tell Colton he was engaged. It was a small town and if he hadn't acted like the giddy groom, their story could be compromised. Obviously, Colton shared that little bit of news with Mason. "Yep, we're just eating breakfast. Er, lunch."

Mason laughed. "Try early dinner. I won't keep you

then. There hasn't been much change in your portfolio since last month. Point two percent increase overall."

"That's good."

"That's below average. I'll shift some stocks around and see if I can get that figure up."

"Sounds good."

"Tell the future wifey I said congrats."

"Will do. Thanks, Mason."

"Yep. Keep your nose clean. And whatever you have going on with Ward, put that shit to bed."

"Already planning on it."

They ended the call, and Blade stabbed a forkful of eggs. His mind was racing with this new information. He needed to figure out a way to get Anna to ditch the case and do it without telling her the real reason why. He got three bites in before she spoke.

"Mason?" The one-worded question was enough. Blade wasn't sure how much he could or even should tell her.

"My financial advisor." Another bite.

"Oil changes pay that much?"

His gaze darted to her, but she had a playful smile teasing her lips.

Blade scooped up more food and swallowed before answering. "I'm not just a mechanic. You know that."

"You're also a hired gun who dabbles in the gaming industry. I guess that's a lucrative way to diversify your assets."

"That's one way to put it." Blade ate the last of his bacon and watched as unanswered questions danced across her gaze.

Finally, she said, "He makes weekend calls. You must be an important client."

Blade sighed, pushing back from the table and crossing

his arms. "We grew up together. He calls on the same date every month no matter the day of the week. He's a little OCD, and I don't mind indulging him. Half the time, I'm busy on an op anyway, and he leaves a message."

"You grew up together? I don't remember seeing that name in your file." She smirked.

He chuckled, relaxing his arms. "You joke, but you're also FBI. I'm sure you've had a very long interesting read at my expense."

"You'd be surprised just how little the bureau knows about you," she said almost too quickly.

He thought about it for several seconds, and said, "Not really surprised, I guess. Colonel torched any and everything there was in the system on all of us. You probably wouldn't even know my eye color if you couldn't see it for yourself."

"That's true. We don't know anything about y'all." The way she said that didn't set well with him, not that he could pinpoint why. It still irked him, and he didn't do well when riled up.

"You know just how much I love fucking you against the shower wall," he snapped.

She gasped as if he slapped her, but he was too irritated to care. "You don't have to be so crude."

"And you don't have to be so cold. You know more about me than anybody." That was true. Not that she knew everything, but she still knew more than most. Yet, she was looking right at him and talking to him as if he was some stranger.

"Are you sitting there telling me your life has been an open book?" she asked incredulously. "Brax, don't play me for a fool." She got up and stormed off.

"Anna!"

The bedroom door slammed. How did that escalate so quickly? Technically, she was right. He wasn't an open book, but that didn't mean he was completely closed off. There was a middle ground he'd stayed in, a middle ground that was already greatly in her favor.

Blade stood up to go after her when his phone rang again. It was Mason.

"Two times in one day, that's a record."

"Just got off the phone with another client. This can't wait."

"Okay," Blade said slowly. "What is it?"

"I have reason to believe you're under federal investigation. I know you take contracts from the government, but you should probably be wary of the feds right now."

"Come again?" he asked, his voice low. There could be any number of reasons the authorities would be looking into him. Had Fletcher Ward finally gotten the right people in his pocket? How would Mason even come across this information?

"They didn't share too many details. Just mentioned a garage in Mayflower Arkansas being investigated. That's a small town. Only one garage I know of there, and I only know about it because of your income. Said they tailed one guy who went out of town while another agent stayed on location to look for clues.

What?

No. Fucking. Way.

This couldn't be right.

No way would Anna be here investigating him. Oh Jesus, did that mean the feds already knew about his connection to Jeremiah's death? If so, she could be here building a case against him. Against him! But if that was true, then why would they be investigating the whole Bang

Shift crew? What happened to Jeremiah went down years before Blade met the guys.

"I take it this information makes sense. Did you see any people following you?"

Anna walked back in the room, her face red as if she'd fought tears. Anger fueled within him. How could she do this? How could she play with his emotions and fucking use him?

"Only the one who was in plain sight."

CHAPTER ELEVEN

Anna splashed water on her face as she fought back the tears. She'd told Blade not to play her for a fool, but in essence, that was all she had been doing. Oh, she loved him.

She freaking loved the man.

But what she was doing for her job happened all behind his back. How could she be angry with him for not opening up when all she was doing was lying? He had every reason not to be forthcoming with her. Reasons he wasn't even aware of. Reasons that gave her the power to ruin his future. A future she'd give just about anything to be a part of.

Truth was she wasn't angry with him. She was mad at herself.

She felt as if she were at a crossroads. Anna either needed to come clean with him, tell him everything, risk losing her job, or worse...get arrested for obstruction of justice.

Or she needed to leave now before she got in too deep.

A humorless laugh escaped her, and she gasped in a sob. In too deep? That happened over six months ago. The time for tough decisions had already passed, and she could no longer live on this borrowed time. She had to make a choice and stick with it. No matter which way she went, there would be consequences.

Another splash of water on her face, and she exited the bathroom. She had to do it now, whatever she was going to do. As she walked into the living room, she changed her mind a half a dozen times. There was no resolve. There was no way to win, and that devastated her.

She knew going in that when everything was said and done, when this mission was over, there'd be no future for them, but she hadn't anticipated just how much this was going to hurt.

"Only the one who was in plain sight," Blade said without any emotion, which felt much more weighted than his tone belied.

She stood at the edge of the room, locked in his steely gaze.

"Thanks, man. I owe you."

Blade tossed the phone onto the couch.

"Who was that?" she asked.

He just stared.

Her heart pounded as her training kicked in. She couldn't help the fact that she instinctively tracked her gun in the room and other things she could use as weapons that lay between her and the pistol. She had to fight the urge to ball her fists to get ready for a physical fight. She didn't believe for one second that Blade would harm her physically, but the daggers he shot her with his angry glare fired off a million warning signals.

"What's wrong?"

And still they stood in a silent standoff.

After what felt like forever, she decided one of them had to make a move. It was dangerous, her relaxing from her stance, but maybe if she made herself less threatening, he'd speak. Anna forced her shoulders to lower, and she crossed her arms before leaning against the wall. It took a lot of effort to make herself appear at ease, and she wasn't even sure if it was believable. Finally, Blade released a growling breath. Not really reassuring, but at least it was something.

"Want to tell me what has you in such a tizzy?" she asked, knowing she was poking the bear, but getting a little irritated anyway.

He laughed, and holy shit, that was the scariest chuckle she'd ever heard. Goosebumps exploded along her arms, and she fought the urge to rub them away.

"What was all that talk about me not opening up to you in Dallas?"

She frowned, not sure how to respond. "I don't remember it like that," She said slowly. "I remember me doing all the talking and later bringing up that I didn't know much about you. Why?"

"Just trying to figure out when the lies started."

He knew. Just how much, she had no idea, but he knew. Jesus, he *knew*.

Her lungs seized, but she did her best to hide her body's reaction.

"What lies?"

"Stop the goddamn games!" he roared.

"Brax—"

"Don't. Don't you dare call me that. I want fucking answers, and I want them right goddamn now, Anna."

"Maybe you should tell me what you're talking about," she barked. She knew she'd kept things from him, but the mission went so deep that she wasn't sure what part he'd found out about.

"I'm talking about the investigation into the Bang Shift. The investigation into *me*."

Shiiit.

"You already know we're under new administration. What Rick said about contracts being analyzed is true. He cannot guarantee work for you guys."

Blade narrowed his eyes. If Anna had to guess, he probably didn't think she was going to say that. Maybe they'd blown off the threat as a formality, and now he understood how real it was. Not that *that* was the biggest part of this. Not by a long shot.

"Then why the pretense? Why not come right out and tell us we could lose government contracts? And why the hell ask for our help if you're not planning on working with us in the future—oh Jesus Christ," he breathed, apparently figuring that part out.

"Yeah, we weren't really looking into the land development company. It was a cover to get your cooperation. We needed to get close and it was an in. I'm really hate this. I do. But this is business. You should at least understand that. You've earned a lot of money off the back of the U.S. government."

"Fuck, Anna, the money is great, but we don't have to have it. Fuck those government contracts. We know how to secure out own jobs."

"Not matter how unsavory," she said, putting her hands on her hips. This was dangerous territory, but they'd started down this road and there was no going back now.

"Yeah, no matter how shitty."

"And just how far would you go, Blade, huh? Just what would you do in the name of justice?"

His face turned to stone before her. Any questions about her theories were just answered...and any suspicions he had about her knowing the truth were just confirmed.

"You know exactly how far I'll go."

"Oh my God," she breathed. "What am I supposed to do with that?" Anna blinked back tears almost as fast as they formed. Thinking he was capable of murder and knowing it outright were two completely different things.

"You know what he did to my sister," he seethed. "I was the one who had to identify her lifeless body. Do you have any idea what that was like?" he yelled. He started pacing, talking to her but seeming lost in his own memories. "But I still did things by the book. I went to the police after I found his goddamn knife where she was killed. I talked to the prosecutor about everything. And you know what, his fucking daddy gave him an alibi. He walked around town, threatening to do it again. There were two other girls who'd gone missing who lived in the area, Anna. Everyone believed he was behind those, too. Then he threatened my mother." He stopped and leveled a stare. "I didn't do a goddamn thing to him until he showed up on my property, wearing a mask, gloves, and trying to break into her window. Yeah, I probably should have restrained him and called the cops, but he'd killed my sister and was going after my mother just to spite me. So I killed him. With the same blade he used on my sister."

Anna wasn't sure when the tears won out, but they flowed freely now. Both the pain and fierceness were palpable. It was all overwhelming.

"I'm so sorry."

"Not sorry enough that you refused to dig into my past and have me arrested for murder."

"It's not like that," she said quickly. "They don't know anything about your sister." But as soon as she said it, she knew it was only a matter of time. "Why did you go to Ward and Associates that Sunday afternoon?"

Red creeped up his neck. "You followed me?" he asked, but his tone told her it wasn't a question. Might as well get everything out now. There was no more reason to keep him in the dark.

"Yes. And that law firm belongs to Fletcher Ward. I had one of my team members look into it, not knowing it had anything to do with your sister. So even though *I* haven't said anything to the bureau about the Wards, if there's any paper trail left that Colonel didn't destroy, someone is going to make the connection. It's only a matter of time."

"Colonel didn't leave anything. If he had, I'd have been thrown behind bars a long fucking time ago." He took a frustrated breath. "Were you ever going to tell me what's going on, or was I just going to wake up in handcuffs one morning?"

"I don't know," she breathed. "I've been battling with that decision from the beginning, and after the phone call I got this morning about the connection to you and Fletcher Ward, I've been thinking about it nonstop."

"Except when you let me fuck you after we got up."

She refused to be baited. It was time for answers, and she wasn't sure how much longer this window would be open. "Did you hurt Mr. Ward? Is that why you went there, because the bureau's been looking for him, and he's been M.I.A.?"

"So now you think I'm a cold-blooded killer?"

How dare he act offended.

"Jesus, Blade, you're a mercenary! You freaking kill for the highest bidder." That was a low blow. Sure, there was some truth to it, but his job wasn't as sinister as she just made it out to be.

"Get the fuck out of my house," he breathed. Oh shit.

She glanced at the table. Again, an instinctive one, one long ingrained in her.

"You go for that gun, and you won't make it two steps."

She gaped at him. Would he really kill her if she made a move for her weapon?

"Wow, you really don't think very highly of me. The look on your face told me every-goddamn-thing I need to know about you. You don't like me at all. Just enough to fuck before fucking over. Listen here, I might do unsavory things for the almighty dollar, but at least I respect myself enough not to sell my soul by spreading my legs for a case. *Get. Out.*"

Anna walked backward toward the door, knowing better than to turn her back on him. Thankfully, she had her shoes on because, with his mood, she doubted he'd let her pack first, much less slip on some sneakers. Maybe once he had a chance to calm down, she'd be able to come back for her things. She'd go outside and sit on the porch for a bit. This conversation wasn't over, but no way could they talk right now. Once she reached the door, she turned the knob, and whispered, "I'm sorry."

The last thing she heard before she shut the door between her and the man she loved was, "Yes, yes, you are."

THE SECOND THE door closed behind Anna, Blade grabbed his keys and ran out back to his motorcycle. He only had a passing thought that he hoped she wasn't in the driveway when he peeled out. He was furious, but deep down, he didn't want any bodily harm to come to her. Thankfully, she was nowhere in sight when he pulled out.

He lived in a wooded area, and she was probably sitting off among the trees to the side, waiting for him to relax enough to talk. They still had a lot of shit to discuss, and he would find out everything she knew, but right now, he needed to talk to the guys about what he'd found out. The faster they were brought up to speed, the faster they could mitigate the damage.

Within minutes, he was at the garage. Bear was there because the man never took a day off. Blade fired off texts to Roc, Gauge, and Hunter as soon as he dismounted. He wouldn't bother trying to reach Brody. The man was on his way to Eureka Springs for a short honeymoon.

"What are you doing here?" Bear asked. "Better yet, why do you look like someone just killed your puppy?"

"I found something out about the feds. We need to talk. I called the others."

"What's going on?" Bear asked, tossing down the rag he used to clean his hands.

"Rather wait until the others get here, so I only have to say this all once."

"I'll give them five minutes, and then you're talking."

It took three minutes.

As soon as everyone got there, they all filed into the meeting room.

"Shit, let's go outside," Blade said right when he opened his mouth to dive right into the story. It hadn't even occurred to him when he was fighting with Anna that she could have bugged his house. Fuck, he'd need to come clean with the guys just in case some agents were getting his arrest warrant together. If she planned it out just right, they now had irrefutable evidence against him. At least he thought about the threat of electronic monitoring before talking to the guys because, for all he knew, Shelby had been busy planting recording devices all over the garage.

After they walked outside, Blade keep pounding pavement, getting several feet away, well into the parking lot and away from any of their vehicles.

"Rick McMillan is a piece of shit."

Bear crossed his arms as the other guys shifted, looking confused. "Explain," their fearless leader said.

And so Blade did. He told them what he'd learned from his source—not naming Mason by name—and confronting Anna, who hadn't denied it. The story was followed by a litany of curses by everyone in the group.

"Jesus, I'm sorry, man," Hunter said.

The sympathy in his eyes fueled Blade's anger all over again. "Fuck her," he said sharply. If she could investigate him behind his back, he never really knew her anyway.

Still hurt like hell, though.

"Sorry, but this doesn't make sense," Gauge said. He was the only one in the group with official law enforcement training, hell he was an agent himself. "That's a lot of trouble just to look into our group when we hadn't done anything to instigate the investigation. Ops take funding. The last thing the bureau is going to do is throw money at something that isn't a sure thing."

"Maybe there's a political reason? The government loves a good PR," Hunter said.

"Fucking politicians," Roc grumbled.

"Well, I have a theory," Blade said slowly. "I can't be sure, but I think I might be the target of the investigation." He ran a hand through his spiked hair. "Colonel got rid of some damning shit on me. I know they're trying to find just how bad it was."

"Shit, I'm sure it was bad on all of us," Hunter said, and rubbed the stubble on his chin.

"Well, my source told me they were looking into me. And, uh, if they got enough evidence, I'm going to fry." They all stared at him, waiting. "I've never told anybody this." He laughed without humor. "Except the woman who's going to put me away." He shook his head. "Jesus, this is so messed up." Taking a deep breath, Blade told them the story of his sister's murder and the guy who did it, not leaving anything out.

"You sure it was him?" Bear asked.

"Yeah, I found his knife at the crime scene. He left it like a calling card just for me." He reached into his waistband where the knife was usually secured in his pants and cussed. "I usually carry it with me, but I was a little too distracted when I bolted. Anyway, his initials used to be on it, but they're worn off."

"That's not much evidence," Gauge said.

"Yeah, I also overheard him confess to the killing one night when he was out with my cousins. When I confronted him, he bragged about it and called me stupid for not figuring it out when he'd left the knife. I went to the police. I tried my damnedest to get him arrested. Nothing. When I wouldn't let the investigation go, that's when he got pissed and threatened my mother."

"Sounds like you did the world a favor," Roc said, almost bored.

"We need to get to the bottom of this," Bear said, and pulled out his phone.

"What are you doing?" Blade asked.

Bear didn't respond, just put it on speaker.

"McMillian."

Blade glared at Bear. What the hell was he doing calling Anna's boss?

"I hear you've decided to pry into our lives." Bear tsked. "That's not being a team player."

Rick was quiet for a few seconds. "What have you heard?"

"Fuck. That. Do you seriously expect us to show our hand first?"

There was rustling around on the other end of the phone as if he was shoving papers away and closing a door. "Look," he whispered. "It wasn't my idea. Another agency is investigating some guy with a very loose connection to one of your men."

What a weasel. Even Blade could tell the man was lying through his teeth.

"Bullshit."

"No, not completely anyway." He sighed. "What I told you about funding is true. What I told you about the other agency is also true. In fact, those guys are leads on this investigation. Not the FBI."

"What's the agency?"

"I can't tell you that. Who told you about the investigation?"

"Get bent. I ain't telling you shit."

"Look, the fact that you know what you do is enough to get me in a boatload of trouble. Work with me here."

"No way. As of this moment, your agents are out. They better be gone from this town within the hour and we better not find them before that. Don't call us to do shit for you."

"Don't hurt—"

Bear hung up on him.

"God, I'm so sorry," Blade said. This was all his fault.

"Don't even go there," Bear said. Then he turned to Gauge. "I hate to ask, man, but you have a choice to make. As of this moment, we are done working with the government. You're either with us or against us. We go way back, so I'll give you a choice and a head start if you pick the wrong one."

Gauge lifted his hands in a placating gesture. "I have a better retirement plan in the private sector."

"Good." He turned to the rest of the guys. "C'mon. We have a shop to clean." And he didn't mean the floors. "Then we need to find out just how much our little agent friend knows."

CHAPTER TWELVE

AFTER BLADE LEFT, Anna contemplated going back into the house to pack a few of her things. She was not going to leave town without talking to him, but she figured she should stay at the safe house until he was ready to discuss everything. For all she knew, he needed a couple of days to stew.

She just hoped she had a couple of days left. If Rick and her team figured anything out about Blade's sister and Jeremiah Ward, she'd be yanked off this mission...either for some incompetency reason for not figuring it out after being so close to him, or for withholding crucial information pertinent to the case. Whichever reason, it didn't look good for her. And if she wasn't allowed to stay in the circle, she wouldn't know what happened to Blade until the agents made their move. She needed to figure out a way to resolve this mess and do it quickly before Rick discovered anything more.

Her phone rang, and she groaned when she saw her boss's name pop up.

"Hello?"

"I want you on the first plane back."

Oh no. He couldn't have figured it all out already. "I still have—"

"This isn't a debate. I just got off the phone with Bear, and they know we were there to look into them. The mission is compromised, and I can't guarantee your safety anymore. Not that you're safe from me! Care to tell me how that happened?"

Jeez, word traveled fast. She hadn't thought he'd contact the feds. Anna had assumed he'd avoid them as much as possible, more so than he wanted to avoid the one currently sitting on his porch. She could either lie, or she could pull up her big girl panties and face the music. Losing her job wouldn't help Blade at all, but she was tired of all the secrecy.

"He confronted me."

Rick exploded, spewing profanities that would make a sailor blush. He ranted about her knowing how to do her job, this not being led by them, even dropped words like obstruction of justice. Anna sat there, taking it all in. Everything he said, she deserved to hear. When he took a breath, she opened her mouth to explain herself, but he was just sucking in air to yell some more.

"We have a face-to-face meeting tomorrow morning. I want you here. More importantly, they want you gone. I don't think they were serious about causing you harm, but we're not taking chances."

What did he mean by that? Blade had told her he wanted her out of his house, but he wouldn't hurt her. Not really.

The emotional pain he inflicted did more damage anyway.

"Yes, sir." The first words she'd gotten to say since he started his tirade.

Thankful Blade hadn't locked the door, she walked in and started packing her things while Rick continued to berate her. When he paused again, she tried to use the break to clear up some things.

"For the record, I did not tell him anything about the SEC's investigation. They don't know about Mason Showalter. That agency's mission hasn't been compromised."

"I wouldn't even be concerned with that if I were you. You'll be on administrative leave at best. Probably fired. Thrown in jail at worst. You should be focused on your own ass now."

Anna continued to shove clothes in her bags without responding. She knew he was right and couldn't really say anything to argue his point. "I know, sir," she finally said. "But I want you to know, I didn't tell him. I only confirmed it after he found out from another source."

Rick was so silent all of the sudden, even his angry panting had stopped. "What?" he breathed. "You weren't the one to tell him?"

"No." But she would have. She'd been seconds away from coming clean anyway. Someone else just beat her to it. Not that she needed to tell her boss that. She was being truthful, but that didn't mean she had to dig an even bigger grave for herself.

"He received the call from Mason Showalter today. Nothing suspicious about the phone call. I left the room to, um, determine my next move," she continued, again, not lying, "and when I returned he was on the phone again. Whoever was on that call informed him of the mission."

"So you want me to believe there was a second caller? Was there a grassy knoll, too?" he asked sarcastically.

"Actually, I think it's highly possible that the second phone call was with Mason Showalter. I think he either called back or Blade called him after I left the room to continue their discussion in private. I don't know for sure if he was the person on the other end, but it's a viable theory."

"You better hope we can prove you weren't the one to divulge classified information. Maybe you can get a professional slap on the wrist instead of jail time."

"Yes, sir," she muttered.

"Eight o'clock, Fisher. Don't be late."

He hung up the phone, and Anna grabbed her bags. So much for waiting around to talk to Blade. She'd be lucky if she was able to come back in a few days after he'd hopefully calmed down enough for their heart-to-heart. She had damage control with her boss to do now, and no way was he going to wait. As she picked up her toiletry back, she caught the sight of something that glistened in the sunlight on top of the dresser. She walked over to it and picked it up.

It was the knife Blade told her Jeremiah Ward used on his sister. The same one he'd used to kill Jeremiah. Normally, he carried the knife with him, but they hadn't left the house today, and when he did leave a few moments ago, he'd been too preoccupied with her betrayal to get it.

The knife would put him away for good.

Or it could set him free.

She put in in her bag, loaded up the car, and headed to the safe house to get the suitcase she had there. She'd decide later what she would do with the knife.

Shelby wasn't anywhere to be found, so she tried calling her to tell her what had gone down. Rick hadn't specifically said he wanted her back, too, but she figured they were both being pulled out of Mayflower. It felt like a given.

Shelby didn't answer, but Anna pulled out her work laptop and booked plane tickets for that afternoon for the both of them. She fired off a text to Anna with the link to her confirmation, grabbed her computer, and headed to the rental. She had a few hours before they had to be at the airport.

Plenty of time to talk to Blade.

Oh, she didn't believe for one second he was ready to hear reason...or groveling. But she couldn't leave Arkansas without trying. She backed out of the safe house driveway and headed down the road. As she came up to a crossroad, she reflected how poignant that was. She could continue going straight, taking the path she knew, the one she'd mapped. Or she could toss her plans out the window and take the roads less traveled, the ones bumpy and mess and scary. The ones that made life fun.

She was so lost in her musing that she hadn't noticed the car barreling toward her as she came up to the intersection. Anna slammed on her brakes and turned the wheel, hoping for a lesser impact than one straight on. She screamed as they slammed into each other and skidded across the road, her car landing in the ditch.

There goes the deposit. As if I'm not in enough trouble.

She groaned as she pried the door open and got out. She walked toward the van, a late 70s model built like a tank sporting barely a scratch. She glanced back at the road, noticing there weren't any stop signs. That was a dangerous thing, even out in the country where there wasn't a lot of traffic.

"Hello?" she called out as she approached the van. She peeked into the window as she neared, but didn't see anyone. Worried they might not have been wearing a seat belt and were hurt, she rushed to the door and yanked. It flew open and out of her hands. She gasped, but someone in the shadow covered her face with a blanket. Anna screamed and twisted, making noise as she quickly tried to extricate herself from the cloth.

From the assailant.

"Hurry," someone said, telling her with just one word whoever this was wasn't acting alone. Some kind of rope was wrapped around her, securing the blanket over her face, before she was thrown onto the floor of the van. Oh God, she was going to suffocate. Anna wiggled as best she could, trying to create space within the makeshift hood.

Ripping sounds made her freeze, and then there was a hole right were her mouth was.

"That'll keep you alive for now," the person said. It wasn't a voice she recognized, but she was grateful whoever it was hadn't planned on killing her right away. She hadn't heard of kidnappings or human trafficking being a major problem in this area, but in her line of work, she knew it was possible anywhere.

It sounded as if the door opened again, and Anna lay very still to pick up any sounds she could. Anything she could figure out could be the key to saving her life. After several seconds, something landed right by her face and she gasped.

"Careful with her computer. I want to have one of my guys look at it."

Crap, they took her things from the car. She shouldn't be surprised by that. Criminals typically exploited all forms of illegal activity.

"Maybe there's something on it that'll tell us how much she knows."

Oh no. No, no, no, no. This wasn't some random kidnapping and robbery. He not only knew she had a computer, but he wanted to know what she actually had on it. This wasn't a wrong-place-wrong-time type of thing.

She was targeted.

Out of all the cases she'd worked, she'd taken down a lot of people and had crossed even more.

The one that hurt the most was the one she'd tried to clear the air with today.

A deep sense of foreboding enveloped her. He'd told her to get out. Rick had said they'd wanted her gone.

"Well now, what's this?" the only one talking said, but she had no idea what he was talking about, and he didn't elaborate. After several seconds, he said, "Have the car towed to the shop."

The shop? Could Blade be behind this? Would he kidnap her to secure his freedom? Those men were capable of a lot. She could only imagine what all they'd done that the government had given them a blank check to complete.

And that was without any threat to their operation. People did all kinds of stuff when their livelihood was threatened.

She didn't want to believe that, but there was a part of her that refused to dismiss any theories at this point.

Even ones that would totally and completely destroy her.

CHAPTER THIRTEEN

"I'm sorry you had to cut your trip short," Blade said as Brody walked into the shop the next morning. He was dead on his feet, not having slept at all. Anna had packed everything and left, not leaving a trace she'd ever been at his house. He knew he'd told her to get out, but there was a small part of him that hoped she'd been stubborn enough to stay and hash it out. Only because he wanted more answers.

That was the only reason he'd allow himself to accept.

"It wasn't a trip. It was a honeymoon," Brody clarified with a glare.

Blade winced.

Brody clapped him on the back. "Once we get this mess cleared up, and I know my family is safe, I'm going back and I'm not taking my phone, dude."

If Blade felt like shit before bringing this mess down on everyone, risking their business and their lives, he felt like the scum of the earth now. "I won't let anything happen to your family."

Brody grabbed him by the shoulders, so he'd face him

head on. "I was talking about you. You're my family, too. I'm not letting you go to jail for what happened."

Blade was speechless. Yeah, he still had some of his family left, and actually remembered his childhood, unlike Brody, but this man right here was the brother he never had.

"Thanks. I still owe you."

"You're goddamn right you do. On my fucking honeymoon," Brody muttered as he walked toward the meeting room. "I take it y'all have swept for critters?"

"No bugs," Bear said. "We checked everywhere. Just the same, we have a white noise machine running throughout the building."

"You didn't find any or you got rid of them?" Brody asked.

"There were none," Gauge said.

"That doesn't make any sense. Why scope out the shop, put an agent on location, and not record everything going on?"

"Yeah, we wondered the same thing," Roc said. "The feds are smarter than that. No way would they miss an opportunity to get intel."

"They'd have known our guards would be down. We wouldn't have checked," Hunter added.

"What does that mean?" Brody asked, crossing his arms.

"Not sure," Bear said. "But I think it's possible we're not the main focus of their investigation. Rick said they are working with another agency. The asshole probably tried to milk the opportunity into something more. Hell, for all we know, whatever part we as a group were involved in was off the books."

"Seems complicated," Brody said. "So why even bother?"

"Because they were using me," Blade said. He rubbed a

hand over his face and relayed the story to Brody about his sister, Jeremiah, and even discussed his visit to Colton and how Anna asked him about Mr. Ward. He left nothing out, wanting Brody to know about everything he'd told the rest of the guys yesterday.

Brody watched silently, remaining quiet once Blade finished. When he opened his mouth, his words bit harder than what he assumed Brody had intended. "Tell me, are you so worked up because the feds might know something about a death resulting from self-defense that happened years ago, or because the woman you love might have betrayed you?"

Blade sucked in a breath.

"You love her?" Roc asked. "Fuck, don't you know better than to think with your little head?"

Blade growled, but Brody grabbed his arm to keep him from advancing on the other man. "Fuck you," Blade barked.

"I think that answers my question," Brody said, shoving Blade so that he sat down on the table beside him. "You need to focus. Attacking our prick of teammate isn't going to do a damn thing."

"Except make me feeling better," Blade seethed.

"Really? You think it'll be that easy?"

And just like that, it was as if the wind had been knocked from his sails. "No. No, I don't," he said miserably.

"I know it's going to be hard, but you have to remain objective. We need to look at every possible angle they can go with this information, and then we need to start calling in favors. I'll be damned if I let them take you down for doing the government's job. Hell, all you did back then was what we do now, except you didn't get paid for it."

Blade opened his mouth to speak, but Bear's phone went off.

The guy checked it and cussed. "It's Shelby." He put it on speaker. "Guess you're not coming this morning," he said with an edge to his voice.

"Your wife's not coming either," she quipped.

Gauge snickered. Bear glared at him, and he raised his hand. "Sorry," he murmured.

"You're lucky I even answered the phone, but I'm curious as why you even have the balls to call after what went down."

Shelby sighed. "Look, I didn't want to do it. I even told Anna this was bullshit, but our hands were tied. Now, Rick is storming around here trying to get an arrest warrant issued."

"Fuck," Blade said. He'd need to scratch pavement and get the hell out of town.

"On what charges?" Bear asked.

"Obstruction of justice. She won't answer her phone. Rick's been trying to reach her all morning. I've tried calling her since last night, but she's not even answering for me. I know y'all are hiding her, but you're making things worse."

"What the hell are you talking about?" Blade asked, the blood in his veins running cold.

"Don't play dumb with me. She booked the plane tickets for both of us yesterday, messaged me with my confirmation, packed her stuff, and disappeared. Anna is on the lam."

"*What?*" Blade roared.

"You heard me."

"No, I didn't because it sounded like you said you don't know where the fuck she is!"

"Um…" Shelby hesitated. "You don't know where Anna is?"

"No. I found out what was going on, confronted her, and told her to get out. After I told the guys, we called Rick and said y'all had to be gone within the hour. I figured she headed back to headquarters."

"Oh shit, you really don't know where she's at?" she asked, but still didn't sound completely convinced. "How do I know you're not lying?"

"That's your department," Roc barked.

"Well if she's not with you, and she's not here with us, where did she go?"

Blade had no idea. One thing was for sure, though, he thought as he bolted up. "We have to find her." Any number of things could have happened, and as the theories flooded through his mind, each one was worse than the previous one.

"I'll check flight records. Maybe she took another plane," Gauge said before jumping up and running to the shop's computer in the main office.

"I'm going to let Rick know she's missing. We'll try to triangulate her cell phone."

Shelby ended the call without warning, and Blade felt like a caged animal, pacing without any direction. She could be anywhere. Anywhere.

"I-I need to go to the house and search the woods."

The door chimed, drawing their attention.

"I'll go take care of it," Hunter said. He rushed out of the room to tend to the customer, but he was only gone long enough for Blade to decide he wasn't sitting around the shop until record searches came back.

"It was a car transporter," Hunter said when he walked in. "It's totaled."

"We'll take care of it later—"

"The paperwork says it's a rental taken out in Anna Sue Fisher's name."

Blade's head whipped around. He started to ask what it looked like, but his feet were already moving before his tongue caught up. He knew exactly what she'd been driving, not that he believed for one second that she took the car out in her own name. She'd have used an alias or put it under a fake company name. He rounded the corner, and came to a screeching halt.

"It's her car."

"How can you tell?" Bear asked, coming up behind him. Blade rushed over to it and looked inside.

"Fuck! There are rabbit feet. It's hers."

"Could be a coincidence," Brody said.

Blade faced him. "She's missing. A car matching the description of the one she was driving was wrecked. It was delivered to our shop. Did I mention she always puts rabbit feet in her vehicles? This isn't a coincidence."

Gauge came into the room. "She didn't book any other flight. If she left town, she drove—what's that?" he asked, pointing to the mangled car that Hunter was inspecting.

"Her car," Blade said.

Gauge cussed and dug out his phone.

"What are you doing?" Brody asked him.

"Calling Rick. We have to treat this like she was taken."

"Who would have done such a thing?" Bear asked. "She's careful. Fuck, the suspects on her case are us, and *we* didn't take her."

"Do you know what this is?" Hunter asked, holding up something. "Found it in the trunk."

"My knife," Blade breathed. The one Jeremiah had used on his sister.

The one he'd left as a calling card to her murder.

Reality slammed into him like a fuck ton of bricks. Only one person had tried to destroy his life since that fateful night. One person who wanted him to suffer. One person who was secretly trying to buy his family land to ruin him in every way possible. One person who must have learned Blade was *engaged*. One person who didn't want Blade to experience any happiness whatsoever.

One person who was going to suffer Blade's wrath.

"I know who has her."

CHAPTER FOURTEEN

Anna awoke with a searing ache pounding in her head. She vaguely remembered her kidnappers trying to shove something down her throat, and when she wouldn't swallow it, they'd knocked her out by force rather than medication. She wasn't a medical expert, but she was certain she was sporting a concussion.

Slowly peeking through one eye to keep from seeing double, she took in her surroundings. It was dark, and it reeked of death. She couldn't make out much with her eyes, but her nose told a story far more frightening in the dark. Someone had died here. At the very least, a dead body had recently been there, whether or not the person had actually taken their last breath there. That did not bode well for her. At all.

As her eyes adjusted to the dim lights, she could make out a table and what looked like the source of the odor. She couldn't be sure the motionless body was dead—for all she knew they'd been knocked out like she was—but she couldn't very well call out to her. She guessed it was a woman with the long hair and skirt.

She very slowly shifted her hands and suppressed a groan of frustration. Unlike the woman across the room, she was tied down. That was a complication she didn't need, not that she fully expected her abductors to toss her into a room without taking extra measures to ensure she couldn't get away. Anna looked down to see how bad it was. She knew how to get out of some knots without any tools. When her gaze landed on something metal, she almost frowned, but stopped herself before she allowed any physical reaction. A metal chair with arms?

She had to look just off the side so her peripheral vision could focus on just what she was tied to. Yeah, it was a chair. She shifted ever so slightly and felt a gentle bounce.

A wheelchair.

Upon closer inspection, it looked as if there was tape on various places—wrapped around the handles under her arms, on the footrest—which didn't make much sense, unless it was a rickety piece of equipment.

Then a flash came to her of her time in Louisiana. A memory...

"...Then he ran it in for a touchdown, yeah. Broken ankle and all."

"It wasn't broken, Lauren."

"Oh please, Justin. Your foot was damn near dangling."

"It was still a hell of a game." Anna would recognize that voice anywhere.

"And a shitty few months after. I had to push you around in that damn wheelchair all over the place."

"Language," Blade's mother said.

"Dude, I remember you taped racing stripes and stuck flags onto that thing." Justin laughed.

"I forgot all about that. Y'all stayed here because your house wasn't wheelchair accessible," Blade said.

Anna's head whipped around and, sure enough, there were old, dirty flags sticking up from the back. "Justin," she breathed.

"Close," someone said. A voice she knew. "Wrong brother, *cher*."

Anna swallowed and looked up quickly, right into Lauren's face. Blade's cousin. A man she'd eaten with and hung out with during her time at Bayou Beasts. "Why?"

"Such a loaded question, *cher*."

"One he's not going to answer," someone else said, coming into view. This person she did not recognize, but the voice matched that of the one in the van when she'd been taken.

"Who are you?"

"Fletcher Ward." Oh, she knew that name. Just never got a chance to put a face with it. Until now. "I only get my hands dirty for a special reason, and Blade is one of them."

Anna schooled her expressions. She didn't have to guess why Mr. Ward wanted to hurt Blade. She knew everything there was to know about that, but she seriously did not understand why Lauren was here or what he had to do with Mr. Ward. Whatever it was, it was bad. Really, really bad.

She glanced around the room again, this time not taking care in being discrete, but there were no clues as to where they'd taken her. She thought quickly, tried to gage the time they'd been in the car, but she had no idea how long she'd been knocked out. She only knew they'd been in the car for a while, but that didn't tell her anything.

"I see your little head is practically spinning. How about a compromise, hmm? I'll let you ask one question if you answer one for me."

She didn't really think she was in a position to deny this request, so she slowly nodded.

"Where's your engagement ring?"

Well, that's not a question she'd anticipated. She frowned, trying to figure out why he'd asked her that and not something to do with the case she'd been working on. The case that got his law practice on the FBI's radar. Or even about Blade since this man knew he was the one to deal the death blow to his son.

"Yeah, that thing's worth a lot of money," Lauren said, yanking her out of her quick musings.

"Patience," Mr. Ward said quickly at him and then looked at her again. "Well?"

"Blade has it." Something told her if she didn't answer this question in a way that they liked, these men were going to end things for her a lot faster than whatever was currently planned. She added quickly, "It was too loose, so he had it sized."

"That's unfortunate," Mr. Ward said. "Do you know where he has it?"

"That's more than one question."

Lauren backhanded her. "You'll answer whatever he asks, *cher*."

She worked her jaw, trying to get feeling back into it. He was out of his mind if he thought she was stupid enough to play along. She'd had lots of interrogation training. She knew how to give nuggets without divulging everything. Not that she got captured often, but the bureau instilled this stuff so much that it was almost second nature how to handle a situation such as this. Did they think they were working with an amateur here?

That's when it dawned on her that they might not actually know she was an agent. Maybe they targeted her because of Blade—that part was becoming obvious—but not because she'd worked with him in an official capacity. These two thought they were really a couple.

They thought she was just some flavor of the week who'd captured his heart.

Thinking of him like that stung a little, but it definitely worked in her favor. These men had no idea what she was capable of. No way was she going to let on.

Anna started crying. It was hard faking big, fat tears, but it was dark. Small ones would do. "P-please don't kill me. I'll—um—tell you whatever I know. Please," she said on an Oscar-worthy sob. But she quickly kept thinking about their motive here. She and Blade had told his family she was an accountant, which could be why they wanted her computer. Not to see classified information, but to find out what she'd calculated on the land valuations and corporate profitability on both Bayou Beasts and Bartholomew Acquired Development.

"Now that's better," Lauren said. Then he rubbed his crotch. Anna had to swallow to keep from vomiting. She didn't have to be a trained special agent to know Lauren got off on the power. She wouldn't be surprised if he had a history of violence against women. Present company excluded.

"Keep it in your pants," Mr. Ward said. "I already have one over there to clean up."

The lady in question still hadn't moved, which confirmed Anna's worst fears.

"Anna, that's Monique. I told you I'd introduce her to the family."

Her stomach rolled. Lauren had mentioned getting back to his date when she was in Louisiana. Had he had this woman the entire time? Anna could only image what all she'd gone through before she drew her last breath.

And if Anna didn't want to have the same ending, she needed to figure out how to get these guys talking…without pissing them off. "Where are we?" she asked.

"The gator cleaning shack on the north end of Bayou Beasts. This area never sees any action, so they focus on hunts to the south. Shack hasn't been used in years."

"Oh, I've used it," Lauren said, and glanced at the lifeless body.

"Shut up, boy." Then he turned to her. "See what I have to put up with? The only son I got left likes pussy cold."

Anna gasped. Lauren was Mr. Ward's son? That meant…

"Yes, Lauren is my bastard child. Barbara and I go way back. I wanted to marry her," he said almost wistfully, "but she married some gas land baron for his money. I did my best to make myself worthy of her love, built the largest law practice in the state." That was an exaggeration. The man definitely had a God complex. "But all she would do was warm my bed every once and a while. After she got pregnant with Lauren, she tried to put a stop to it, but she could never stay away from me. Of course, I had too much dirt on her."

"You blackmailed her," she said, and almost winced for speaking out of turn.

"Yes," was all he said, thankfully not punishing her. She thought back to when Anna met Barbara, but nothing sinister stood out. Then again, she hadn't picked up any weird vibes on Lauren either. She'd been too focused on Blade and how the shame of the engagement made her feel. She knew better than to lose focus. If she hadn't maybe, she'd have learned the truth about his family members and not be stuck here.

"She loved you?" Anna asked softly, trying to gently probe for answers she should've already known.

"With all her heart. Long ago. But she had another boy to take care of. So I got married and had my own child. Their playdates were nice covers for our rendezvouses." He smiled, but it was fraught with sinister glee.

She wasn't sure how to ask this next question without causing anger, but she had to find out. "Did anybody else know about this?"

"Barbara never told anyone. She was too worried her daddy would write her out of the will. That family is known to hold the inheritance over their heads." She'd already learned that from Blade. "She couldn't afford to lose out on the gator income. She'd already lost her husband's income. By the time he'd met his untimely death, the gas wells had run dry. Oh, he'd left her a lot of money, but she wasn't pulling in tons of land royalties each month. I tried to get her to see reason and let us be together out in the open since there was nothing stopping us anymore, but she refused. The little minx had dirt on me, too."

His untimely death. "How did he die?"

Mr. Ward smiled. "That's unimportant." She could press him for answers, but that outcome wouldn't change. Mr. Ward either killed him or was directly involved somehow. If she got out of this alive, she'd report what she knew and let the authorities dig.

And if she didn't get out? Well, then he was right. It was unimportant.

"It's a fucking pain in the ass Bernadette wrote Blade back into the will after I got rid of his daddy."

She felt the blood drain from her face. This man had not only killed Barbara's husband, but also killed Blade's father. Why would he do such a thing? She knew better than to ask that out loud, and really, she knew better than to silently question it, too. He was clearly unhinged.

"Aren't you curious?" he asked with a small smile. That didn't surprise her because that went in line with the God complex assessment she'd already made.

"Yes," she said, feeding his ego.

"Your fiancé killed my boy. All he ever did was love that girl. Of course, I pushed him to get with her. I wanted that family land. Back then, I just knew if Barbara got controlling interest, she wouldn't need that scrawny ass husband of hers anymore. Jeremiah was my ticket to a life with Bernadette. He'd marry Brenna. Lauren was secretly my child. Justin would do whatever his mom and brother wanted." He glared at Lauren. "Of course, I hadn't learned of you and your brother's appetite for submissive women." He shook his head and focused on Anna again. "Things got rough with Jeremiah and Brenna one night. Her death was an accident."

No way did Anna believe that. Not for one second. "How did she die?"

"The little slut like getting cut while fucked. He *accidentally* sliced her throat too deep. He knew how important the plan was. It was never his intention to murder her."

"Not then anyway," Lauren muttered.

Mr. Ward flashed a smile, but didn't comment. Not that she needed him to. They'd planned on killing Blade's sister at some point in the future. Probably shortly after the wedding.

"Yes, well, that plan was no longer viable, and then Blade killed my precious boy," Mr. Ward said, low and menacing. He glanced away as if trying to control his emotion. When he looked back at her, whatever anger had flared was carefully banked. "Blade's father was embarrassed by his son's link to my son's death. Didn't matter that he'd done it to avenge his sister. He'd killed in cold blood. That religious man did not believe that two wrongs made a right. Their relationship was never the same after that." He smiled again.

"So why did you kill him?" she asked, because she assumed he was okay talking about the harm he'd caused Blade—these deaths weren't *unimportant* like Barbara's husband's was.

"I'd made it my life's mission to ruin Blade. The destroyed relationship with his father had been a perk, but I couldn't risk a reconciliation. That would've had both personal and professional implications." Yeah, if Blade and his dad had been able to mend fences, then it'd go against Mr. Ward's agenda to hurt Blade. And any reconciliation could have resulted in Blade being written back into the will. Which made sense as to why this man was angry about Bernadette giving him his rightful inheritance. "With Brenna gone and Blade out of the picture, Barbara would have controlling power through her and her sons. Of course, I'd have made sure there wasn't any threat to her control. Bernadette needed to go, too, once enough time passed. That's the key to not getting caught. You have to spread out the murders."

Oh God, he was going to kill Bernadette. Renewed focus to get out of this alive surged through Anna. She had to break free if only to save Blade's mother. He'd already lost his sister and his father to this madman. All for twisted love and dangerous money.

She looked around the room as she shifted slightly in the wheelchair. There was a door at the other end. If she could quietly lift the footrest, she could lean forward and throw herself against the wall. If she did it just right, with enough downward force on her arm, she could possible break the tape that was wrapped around her wrist. She was going to aim for the side that wasn't her bum ankle. She hoped it wouldn't be an issue, but she didn't want to chance breaking free and screwing it up in the process. That would make running very difficult. She took a calming breath. She'd only have one shot at this.

If she failed, they'd probably kill her immediately.

But if she got just one arm free, she could escape the chair and take these two men down like the badass agent she was. She mentally calculated every possible scenario in preparation for whatever happened as soon as she moved and the men realized what was going on.

Without further hesitation, Anna dropped, putting her plan into motion, but even though she thought of many different outcomes, what happened next wasn't something she'd anticipated.

CHAPTER FIFTEEN

BLADE DIDN'T THINK they'd ever make to his family estate in Louisiana, not that he had any idea where she was within this vast land. She could be tucked away anywhere within these thousands of acres. They'd called Rick and relayed what they'd learned. He and his crew were en route and had contacted the local FBI office for backup. He knew better than to tell them to not get involved. No matter the treachery that had recently come to light, Anna had been there for him and his team. He wouldn't let anyone they worked with get hurt. Especially not the woman he loved more than life itself. Not that he knew how to deal with that. There were a lot of problems to face. Not to mention the fact that it was his love for her that got her into this mess because he knew exactly who it was that took her. It was the one thing out of everything he was sure of—who'd taken her and why.

Mr. Ward had it out for him. Ever since Blade had killed his son, the man had been on a malignant mission, determined to take him down any way possible. Blade should've known Fletcher Ward would've found out about the engagement. Blade had been too focused on Colton divulging something to Anna that he hadn't considered the man would tell his boss the news of his impending nuptials. Not that he believed Colton's actions were sinister. No, Blade figured the guy said something in passing that made its way back to Ward. The only other people who knew about the engagement were his family and the staff at Bayou Beasts, and he trusted them. No one else made sense as the source other than Colton.

"No sign of her here," Gauge said, coming out from the most recent hunting cabin they'd checked. It wasn't as easy as going to the spot where Brenna's body had been found. It had been out in the open for all to see. Nor would Mr. Ward have taken Anna to where Blade had killed Jeremiah. He wasn't aware of the location, and even if he was, it too was in the main yard, out in the open as well. They'd searched the house and talked to his mother when they'd first gotten there. She hadn't seen anything, hadn't been able to provide clues on where to continue the search, so they'd quickly set up a grid pattern and began work, once the house—and technically where the murder occurred— was cleared.

Even though Jeremiah had been killed near the house, his body, though, had been dumped into a small, alligator-infested swamp on the northern side of the property. It had been off-season, so thankfully, there hadn't been any hunters in the area. After he'd given the animals enough time to take care of the body with their sharp teeth and insatiable bellies, Blade harvested them. He hated disposing of what had been perfectly good meat up until then, but he couldn't risk raising animals who'd had a taste of human flesh, nor did he want a hunter taking an animal who'd dined on it. To make sure no more nested in the area, he'd taken a backhoe out there and slowly, over several months, shifted the earth around enough to absorb most of the water. Nature and time took care of the rest.

Thinking of part of the land was bittersweet. He'd been grateful at the time for the small swamp he'd known so well, and also guilty for ruining what had been a viable area for the family business. He rarely went up there anymore. He didn't need the reminder of what he'd done, and it wasn't as if it held any sad memories of his sister. Hell, back then the hunting shed up there was already falling apart. By now it'd be—

He sucked in a lungful of air. "Let's go." He ran for the four-wheeler he'd used to scope out the property. The guys hadn't wanted to use anything motorized like that, preferring to check on foot to keep from alerting Mr. Ward they were in the area, but Blade knew they had too much ground to cover. The element of surprise would've been nice, but they'd have to settle for the element of speed instead.

"Where're we going?" Brody asked through the headset as he raced beside Blade.

"Area Bartholomew Acquired Development wanted."

Why didn't he think of this before? He knew Mr. Ward owned that company. Blade didn't believe for one second the man figured out that was where Blade had disposed of the body. Even though he'd been too young to understand satellite imagery and topography analysis, which in the right hands would be damning evidence against him, Colonel had known what to look for once he'd learned of Blade's shady past. As evil as that man was, it had been nice being on his good side for a while.

Out of the corner of his eye, he saw Brody motion behind him, probably indicting the curve coming up in the road so the others would be caught off guard. Blade could drive these trails blindfolded.

He activated his mic and said, "Just a couple miles this way before we need to kill the engines. We'll go in the rest of the way on foot."

"Glad you're finally seeing reason," Gauge grumbled, obviously pleased Blade was willing to go stealth. Not that he didn't want to rush right up to the door, because he did, but he had a feeling he was going to be right about the shack and didn't want to risk Mr. Ward hearing them coming. Besides, more four-wheelers were coming at the lower end and could be explained away. They didn't have that luxury on the northern portion of the property. Not that Mr. Ward knew that, but it wasn't worth chancing.

They came up to the last bend, and Blade came to a screeching halt. He dismounted and started running through the woods as quietly as possible. A skilled hunter, he knew how to stalk his prey. And he'd come prepared. Not only did he have his knife and gun, but his hand itched to reach for the long blade he'd had since his sister's death resting on his hip. Funny that he'd come to a point in his life where he found comfort in the cold steel that had taken her life.

But he resisted and kept the same quick pace. He knew his teammates were behind him, as were five other guys from the local FBI field office, even though all he heard were the soft noises his own feet made. When the cabin came into view, he slowed, and finally pulled out the menacing-looking knife.

And his gun.

He wasn't an idiot.

He'd long thought he'd use this knife if ever loose ends needing tying, but as he got closer to the door, something deep inside of him knew the need for irony or revenge or whatever had fueled his desire to keep the knife to exact that specific type of justice had faded at some point over the years. Probably once Anna came into his life, and a deeper need took root.

Blade was still angry with her. God, was he ever pissed at that woman. But he hoped more than anything that he'd be given the opportunity to yell at her, demand answers, and fuck her into submission.

"Stand back," Gauge whispered into his headset.

"You can fuck straight off," Blade replied back, inching closer to the door. When he heard voices coming from inside the old wooden shed, he froze and said a silent thank you to the universe for being on his side.

"With Brenna gone and Blade out of the picture, Barbara would have controlling power through her and her sons. Of course, I'd have made sure there wasn't any threat to her control. Bernadette needed to go, too, once enough time passed. That's the key to not getting caught. You have to spread out the murders."

That asshole was planning on killing his mother? New fury boiled inside of him, coupled with relief he'd just seen his mom earlier in the day when they'd arrived on the property, knowing she was safe. But why did that man care if his aunt had controlling interest in the property? He wasn't going to sit out here and hope for an answer to that.

"Everyone in position?" one of the field agents asked. Blade didn't remember those guys' names.

He heard several affirmatives as the officially trained professionals surrounded the building, covering the door and boarded windows.

"On my count."

It happened in a flurry. One second Blade was at the

door, his hand on the knob, the next they'd stormed into the building, crashed though windows, and barked orders to everyone to get down. When Blade busted through, he watched as Anna hit the wall and came crashing down, busting the tape on her wrist in the process.

"Good fucking move," one of the agents closest to her said, voice thick with appreciation. Blade did his best not to put that man on the ground as he shoved him out of the way to get to her.

"Baby," he breathed as he reached for her, all the while she was struggling to get up.

"Brax," she murmured on a sob.

It crushed him to see her tears. Jesus, he'd never seen her cry before. She was a tough as nails little spitfire, and seeing her emotions on display like this made him want to change his stance on not gutting the man who took her. Slowly, painfully.

He helped her tug on the tape to free her other hand and pulled her into his arms. He heard the commotion around him as they rounded up Mr. Ward and anybody else in the cabin.

"She's dead," Hunter said.

Blade's head whipped around. The sunlight streaming in, landing on a blond woman, frail and bloody. The same size and hair color of his sister. Memories assaulted him of her lifeless body and he squeezed Anna in his embrace as he fought to maintain control.

"Don't touch her!" someone yelled, the sound of the voice sending chills down his spine.

"Lauren?" Blade asked. "What the fuck?"

Lauren paid him no attention. He screamed some unintelligible words as he tried to rush the officer inspecting the poor woman's head. Not that he got far. Two other agents were holding him down. Several of his guys had Mr. Ward on the ground.

"Your mom," Anna said almost in a panic. "They're planning on—"

"She's fine. She was here when we showed up. Sent her away."

"They talked about your aunt. I'm not sure if she's on the level."

Fear washed over him, knowing his mom could have gone to her house. Hell, if not, she'd have called her to tell her what was going on at the estate. Blade dug out his phone as he helped Anna stand. Then he rushed outside for better lighting. A helicopter flew overhead as he hit the button to call his mom.

"Hello?"

"Oh thank God. Where are you?"

"At Barbara's. We were—"

"Get away from her," he yelled.

"Why?" she asked slowly. "We're in town and she drove."

"Something's going on. Not sure who all you can trust. Are you in a crowded area?"

"Yes. We're at Boudreau's, Barbara's favorite restaurant."

"Jesus Christ, don't eat anything."

"What's going on?" Brody asked, coming up next to him.

Blade quickly explained to him that the younger guy in the shed was his cousin and his mom was currently out with his aunt. Brody rushed back in the building to tell one of the local feds, so they could get someone out there to protect her.

"Listen to me, Mom. Don't eat anything. Don't leave

with her. Don't do anything. They're sending an officer to you."

"Are you going to explain what's going on?"

"Yeah. Just as soon as I figure this shit out myself."

He stayed on the phone with his mom until a deputy arrived at the restaurant and took Barbara in for questioning, but while he waited not-so-patiently for help to arrive, Anna had come outside to tell him what all she knew.

And what she told him blew his quiet little family life wide open. Barbara and Mr. Ward. Lauren. All those deaths. Not that his life had been so strait-laced before, but Jesus Christ, his family was all kinds of fucked up! And knowing the truth, the enormous reality, it only exemplified all the reasons he wasn't worthy of the woman sitting beside him.

The love of his life was safe.

His sweet momma was safe.

He didn't need to push his luck anymore. He was better off living the closed off life he had before she'd ever walked into it. Not that she ever wanted to be a part of his life anyway. She'd played him, and he'd been the fool thinking she'd reciprocated his feelings. A part of him believed that she did care about him on some level, but she didn't feel the same way about him as he did her. She'd proven she loved her job more than anything in this world.

"I owe you an apology," Anna said. "For everything."

He sighed and rubbed a dirt roughened hand over his face. "Me, too. But really, sweetheart, it doesn't even matter anymore." With that, he stood up, trying not to focus on her shocked expression because it would only test his resolve. "Take care of yourself. Please."

Then he walked away. Away from happiness. Away from his heart.

CHAPTER SIXTEEN

Anna sat in the meeting room of her assigned field agency following the disciplinary meeting. It had been scheduled after her administrative leave had lapsed. Because of the work she'd done linking several unsolved mysteries to Lauren's confession and the fact that she hadn't been the one to leak information to Blade, the hearing had been more of a formality than anything else. She'd still hated the time away. She'd used that forced vacation to both recuperate and reflect since she couldn't do much else. Seeing as she wasn't that injured coming out of the kidnapping, one of those was much easier than the other. She mended quickly. She did *physically*, anyway.

The other thing she focused on wasn't as successful. Reflecting on everything didn't give her any answers. Blade never once reached out to her, and she'd been prohibited from making contact with him until after the administrative hearing...if then. Anna had considered ditching the tail the FBI put on her and making a quick trip to Arkansas, but she figured she didn't need to push it. If she knew beyond the shadow of any doubt that she could get Blade to talk to her, she might have felt differently, but she realized he was coming to terms with a lot of betrayal. She just wished she didn't have to be a part of all that.

"Hey, hey, look who it is," Carson said as he walked in, dragging her out of her thoughts of Blade and the next step she was going to take. He walked over and hugged her before taking a seat. "How's it going?"

"Good." Because that was the acceptable answer.

Viola gasped when she walked in. "There you are! How'd it go?" She rushed over and hugged Anna.

"Good." Again, it was the answer she wanted to hear. Anna would get a chance to elaborate soon enough.

Rick walked in, gave her a nod, and sat. He already knew the outcome of the hearing. He'd been there with her. For all the growling around that man did, he knew how to have his teammates' backs. She had a greater appreciation for him now more than ever.

Shelby and Darrell walked in next and stopped whatever they were chatting about when they saw Anna. Shelby smiled. Darrell made a sound that could either be interpreted as a greeting or disapproval. Either one was totally possible where he was concerned.

"As you all can see, we have a guest with us today," Rick said, and eyed Anna.

This was the part she wasn't looking forward to.

"Guest?" Carson said with a laugh that slowly died. "Oh, shit."

"Indeed," Rick said. "Anna Sue Fisher is being reassigned."

"What? Viola said. "That's not fair! She didn't do *anything* wrong."

"To Arkansas," Rick said with a smile.

Everyone realized at different moments what that meant. Shelby was the first, and she flat out giggled.

"You *wuuuv* him."

"Stop it," Anna muttered through a smile. It didn't matter how she felt about Blade. She knew she had her work cut out where he was concerned. But it wasn't as if she could afford to change careers. Since the inquiry into Mason Showalter was still in full force, she'd posed the idea to Rick as sort of a peace offering. She'd be willing to transfer to another field office and he wouldn't have to risk Anna breaking his trust. She couldn't tell Blade about the case if she wasn't working on the team.

Although she was sad to be leaving the people she'd been working with for years.

"Anna will be tasked with closing what cases she can that can be definitively linked to Laurent Mahoney. As you all know, he confessed to thirteen murders. He admitted he and Jeremiah Ward committed the first two together. After Ward's death, Mahoney continued the tradition in a psychotic tribute to his dead brother."

"Jeez, that's messed up," Carson said.

"Yes. Apparently, the first one was an accident. Happened the night Laurent found out about his true parentage. Jeremiah told him, and he went into a rage. After, they did it again on the anniversary of their newly discovered brotherhood. He's done it every year since."

"Are we sure Brenna Young was one of those commemorative victims?" Viola asked.

"Yes. Though we don't have a corroborating witness. Just his statement of the events." Anna hadn't been allowed to be there for the confession. What work she'd been allowed to do on those cases, she'd done remotely and technically off the record. Now that she was fully reinstated, she could officially work on closing those cases.

"Poor Blade. I couldn't even imagine the pain he must be going through," Shelby said.

"He's still a mercenary," Rick said. Nothing had really changed on his feelings regarding the Bang Shift. Not that the agency had been able to find anything on those men. Rick had to accept the fact that whatever Colonel had destroyed had disappeared forever. If he wanted to sever ties with them, he'd need to come up with something new. And he did want to destroy all connections. For some reason, he had a major dislike for those men. Didn't seem to matter much anyway. The moment those guys learned the truth about the mission Anna and her team were on, they'd effectively stopped all communication. The breakup hadn't been with just her, but she had a feeling she was the only one using the power of ice cream to deal.

"Jack Parsons doesn't seem to care," Carson said. Anna had heard about that. Jack had worked with the Bang Shift long before Rick's team ever did, and he was furious of the mess Rick had made of that working relationship. If anyone could mend fences between the government and that contracted group, it would be him. She wasn't holding her breath, though.

"You want to work RICO? I've already transferred one agent today. I can make it happen."

"No," Carson said quickly. "Jack's a dick. I'll keep my happy ass here."

"Agreed," Darrell said.

"So where does this leave us with the SEC?" Shelby asked.

Rick's gaze flashed to Anna before answering. "We'll discuss that later."

"Don't mean to be an ass," Darrell said, "but you do know she's going to make contact with Blade Young once she transfers."

"She's sitting right here," Anna said, deadpan.

He lifted his hands and leaned back. "Just stating the obvious. He has an unidentified link to Mason Showalter, a key party to an ongoing investigation.

"A flimsy link at best," Anna countered.

"Still." Darrell shrugged.

"Anna is aware of the consequences if she were to discuss any classified intel with someone outside of the agency."

Yes, she was. The committee had made it abundantly clear this morning that she'd be terminated if she breathed a word of anything to anyone. "And I plan on being around and making a difference in the lives of people for many years to come."

Darrell stared at her for several seconds before finally nodding. She didn't have to convince him, but she didn't want her teammates—former teammates—to think she'd do anything to hinder their investigation.

She had no intention of doing that.

Then again, she also had no intention of keeping Blade in the dark either. She hadn't figured out how to tell him the main reason behind the investigation, why he'd been the one they'd wanted Anna to work with. But one thing she'd decided when doing all of that reflecting while on leave was that there would *not* be any more secrets between them. There had to be a way Anna could be honest with Blade without breaking the trust of her colleagues.

She hadn't quite figured that part out yet, and with just a week to pack and move before she had to report to her new boss, she was quickly running out of time.

———

HE KNEW IT WAS A DREAM.

Only, this time, the sweet smell of rose petals wafting through his nostrils overpowered the phantom scent of lavender. He used to never understand why a seventeen-year-old girl wanted to smell like flowers as his sister had once loved, but then he met Anna and her love of rose-scented lotion give him a whole new appreciation to floral scents. Unlike Brenna's love of purple, Anna didn't have a preference for all things red. She just loved the smell of roses. Maybe it was a teenage thing to associate the color with the flower. He didn't know, but there was no mistaking Anna's love for the aroma.

It was why he'd kept a fresh bouquet by his bed. When it was the last thing he smelled before falling asleep, the nightmares of lavender and blood stayed away, and images of Anna Sue Fisher engulfed him.

It was a completely different type of nightmare than what he'd had all those years. That woman haunted his dreams, and like a damn fool, he craved it, fed it. Of course, he still dreamed about his sister. Not all the time. But when he did, it was different than before.

The scent of lavender tickled his nose right before the young girl appeared. Peaceful. So completely unlike the recurring dream he'd had for all those years.

"Where's Jeremiah?"

He knew his sister was going to ask that, because she always did. That was the one part that never changed.

And his answer never deviated still. "In Hell."

"Was it you?" she asked as tears welled in her lifeless eyes.

"Yes."

It was then she looked at him, and the dull emptiness of her gaze shifted, warmed. "Thank you."

He awoke, the last images of his smiling sister fading into the early morning light.

Followed by an ache in his head he wished he'd get used to.

"Damn tequila," he muttered as he tossed the sheets off him and sighed. Drowning his sorrows in liquor wasn't the answer. Hell, it didn't even dull the pain anymore. Not that he was still hurting over the loss of his sister. He'd always love her, and since Mr. Ward had been put behind bars and Lauren's role discovered, it was as if he'd attained a certain amount of peace where his sister's death was concerned. And on some level, she did too. It had been a log fifteen years in the making, but he felt she was finally at rest. It was somehow closure for them both.

So, yeah, the ache he tried to kill had nothing to with her. It had been created by Anna Sue Fisher.

It was always Anna. The woman gutted him, and the worst part was he *knew* why. He'd always known, even when he'd told himself he didn't understand the spell she'd put him under.

He loved her.

Blade wasn't sure when it happened. Probably shortly after meeting her when she'd first come to town working undercover as extra protection for Xan. He wouldn't be surprised if it had been love at first sight, but he'd been so wrapped up in his own nonexistent life to notice.

Groaning, he got up, downed some Ibuprofen, brushed his teeth, and got in the shower. He needed to get to the shop and finish working on the El Camino that had been neglected since Shelby left. Jeez, they sure could use her help. The woman was a wiz under the hood. She knew her shit better than some of the mechanics they'd hired over the years. He hated how things went down with the feds. Not only were the guys not ever planning on working with them again, they couldn't risk continuing any friendships either. They'd severed ties with Shelby...with everyone.

Including Anna.

Making quick work of getting clean, he got rinsed off and got out, thoughts still focused on her. He toweled himself off as he walked down the hall, so focused on her that the phantom scent of roses grew stronger with every passing second. When he walked into his bedroom, he froze.

"Good morning," Anna said. She lay on his bed, propped up on her elbows, legs crossed in front of her.

He momentarily wondered if he'd gone completely crazy and was now seeing things in addition to smelling them. But he knew if he'd been imagining her on his bed, she wouldn't be wearing clothes.

"What are you doing here?"

She smiled. "What? Not 'How did you get in here?' You might want to cover up." Her gaze traveled down his body, zeroing in on his exposed manhood.

He cussed and quickly wrapped the towel around his waist.

She pouted, and it was the cutest little face. He almost smiled...until he felt blood stirring in his groin at the sight of her on top of his sheets.

"What are you doing here?" he asked again, almost angry. He definitely wasn't happy about his body's reaction to her.

She sat up a little, leaning toward him, although he was still across the room.

"I wanted to tell you in person that I'm being transferred."

"Where?"

"Here."

He blinked, letting her words sink in. Many words and questions flew in his mind, but he'd only let his mouth utter one. "Why?"

"Several reasons. One being that I can't be trusted to work on an ongoing investigation."

"Why the hell not?" he asked, pissed that anybody would question her ability as an agent. Fuck, she was so good at it that she'd fooled him into thinking she cared about him beyond an assignment. She had drive. That was one thing nobody, not even himself, could question.

She sighed as she stood. "If I tell you, I could get into a lot of trouble. Like, seriously, if the powers that be find out I even mentioned a tiny bit of this to you, I'd be out of a job. Maybe even thrown in jail."

"What?" he asked, moving forward for the first time since entering the room.

She took a deep breath, glancing up from the corner of her eye. "I was tasked with working directly with you."

His heart pounded a little. She hadn't said anything he hadn't already considered, but having her confirm it didn't feel good. How much had the feds already known about his involvement in Jeremiah Ward's murder? If she hadn't already told him she was here because she'd been reassigned, he'd think she was here to arrest him. That would've been the fucking cherry on this messy-ass cake.

"I see," he said through tight lips.

"No, baby, you don't." His shoulders tensed at the endearment, but he didn't say anything, waiting on her to continue. "We weren't working with the IRS. It was another federal agency."

"I'm aware of that. Rick informed us that day you'd been kidnapped."

She nodded slowly. He could practically see the wheels turning in her head. "Did he say it was the SEC?"

"The SEC?" he asked, taken aback. What would the SEC want with him?

"I'll take that as a no." She paused, watching him, and he realized just how hard this was for her. Unable to resist the need to ease her fears, he took a few more steps, closing the distance between them. He didn't sit on the bed, though. He couldn't be that close to her. Instead, he leaned against the dresser. "The original case had nothing to do with you specifically. We're—they're—investigating a man named Mason Showalter."

That was the last thing he expected her to say. "Mason? Why?"

She shook her head before he finished his short question. "I honestly don't know, but even if I did, I couldn't tell you. The fact that you know a friend of yours is currently under federal investigation is already too much."

"I'm technically just a client of his." Blade shrugged. "I mean, we were friends when we were younger, but we lost touch. Once I started getting land royalties again, I needed some investment advice. I'd heard he was good with that sort of thing. We've only recently reconnected. It's not as if we go fishing together or anything. Cordial conversations while we conduct business is about the extent of it."

Anna nodded at that. "My assignment was to get close to you and see what kind of relationship you had with him."

Another confession that burned. "Mission accomplished. You could've just fucking asked rather than playing me. You got your answer inside of thirty seconds by just bringing it up." He understood if she was on assignment asking him outright would not have been an option. She didn't know how loyal he was to Mason. But just because he understood why she couldn't do that didn't mean he liked the fact she used his feelings for what amounted to the advancement of her career.

She narrowed her gaze. "Do you think I *wanted* to keep you in the dark? It *killed* me not being open with you." She blinked as if fighting tears. "Brax, there hasn't been a day that's gone by since we got back from Dallas that I haven't thought about you."

His name on her lips had his cock hardening. Her admission, though, that had his heart swelling.

She stood before he could say anything, not that he was sure he could manage words as all the blood in his body rushed south. The look in her eyes—naughty with a hint of mischief—was not helping the situation. In about two seconds, this damn towel around his hips would be tenting.

"Remember how that night started?" she asked. He didn't remember the exact starting point, but as she yanked the towel away and dropped to her knees, it didn't take a genius to figure out what she'd been talking about.

"Fuck, Anna," he breathed as she took him into her mouth. His hands dove into her hair, and he tried his best not to fist it around his knuckles. But good lord, he couldn't concentrate as she sucked him into the back of her throat. He'd forgotten how good she was at this, which he tried not to think about why that was. At least he got to reap the benefits. "Oh, yeah," he murmured when her throat relaxed enough for him to sink all the way in. She grabbed his hips and pulled, signaling she wanted him to thrust rather than staying still. He did it almost involuntarily and then eased back before pumping slowly into her mouth. "You like that?"

She nodded around his dick and, all too soon, he felt the tale-tell tingling sign at the base of his spine. As much as he'd love to finish this way, he wanted something more. For the first time since she started, he gripped her hair and pulled. She groaned, giving him that cute little pout that he loved, but it didn't stay on her face for long. As soon as he scooped her up, she gasped out a surprise and then a giggle as he dropped her on the bed.

Her laughter died down as he yanked her shorts off and buried his face between her legs. So fucking sweet. Her scent had him aching more than her mouth had, and Blade had to fight the urge to hump her leg as he licked her pussy. Not roses. Woman. All woman.

All his.

God, he could devour her for hours. He nibbled on her lips and teased her clit. Within minutes, she was moaning and wiggling her hips, trying to get him to focus on her clit. He knew as soon as he did, she'd go off, but he wanted to drag it out as long as he could.

"Please, please," she started chanting as her fingers found his hair. The forceful little minx was having none of the teasing, so he relented and gave her what she wanted. Right as she sucked in a lungful of air, he shoved a finger inside of her and rubbed as he drew the neediest little spot on her body into the warm cavern of his mouth. When she screamed, he almost smiled triumphantly.

Then he realized she'd been making the demands, and like an eager young man, he'd given her whatever she wanted. It wasn't as if he'd coaxed her to give him what he wanted.

Not that he hadn't enjoyed every second.

Before she came down off her high, Blade dug out a condom from his nightstand, rolled it on, and pushed into her. He groaned when he felt her walls flexing around him.

"So good," he whispered into her ear. She moaned and grabbed onto his back, not even trying to verbally reply. He was fine letting her body do the talking.

Blade kissed her neck, her chest, her breast. His mouth landed everywhere he could reach almost in desperation to taste her everywhere. All the while he thrust into her over and over, increasing in speed until he was mindless with need. From the incoherent sounds she was making, he figured she was right there with him. If not, he was glad she'd already come once because he didn't think he could hold off much longer.

"Oh, God," she groaned, hitching her legs up higher, locking them around his back. "Gonna make me come."

Jesus Christ, that did it. Blade dug his head into her neck and pounded into her. He was vaguely aware of the screams ripping from her throat. His answering roar drowned everything else out as he came harder than he ever had in his life.

Even after he emptied all he had to give into the condom, he continued to pump slowly, not wanting to pull out. She felt too good, and he didn't just mean sexually.

When he could no longer put it off, he gently extricated himself, took care of the protection, and eased back into the bed, taking her into his arms. He didn't want to think about anything other than this moment with her, but other stronger needs took over. Needs that had nothing to do with the physical and absolutely everything to do with the emotional pull she had on him.

"Tell me what you being here means."

She looked up at him, and the air locked in his lungs. He'd never seen her gaze so open, so trusting.

"I love you," she barely whispered.

He smiled, his heart that had swelled earlier with warm, precious feelings damn near exploded. "I love you, too, babe," he said, and kissed the top of her head because he just couldn't keep his lips off her. "Where does that leave us?" he asked into her hair.

"I guess it leaves us seeing where this goes."

"I already know where it goes," he said, and even though he hated it, he nudged her up and slipped out of the bed.

"Where are you going?" she asked. He didn't miss the slight panic in her voice she hadn't been able to hide.

Blade suppressed a smile as he opened his drawer and pulled out the item he was after. When he turned to her, he hid it in his hand so she couldn't see what he had until he was ready.

"Anna Sue Fisher," he started, and tugged on her left hand. It wasn't until he had her fingers in his grasp that she saw what he'd gotten.

She gasped.

He let the smile free he'd been holding back as he placed his grandma's ring on the tip of *that* finger. "I will never feel worthy of your love, but if you'll be my wife, not a day will go by where you won't know how much you are loved. I promise to cherish you forever." That was true whether or not she married him, but as he waited for her answer, he'd never been so anxious to hear that one little word.

"Yes." She smiled the biggest smile he'd ever seen from her. "Yes," she said louder, and threw her arms around him. "Yes, yes, yes, yes."

They still had a lot of things to discuss, but they had the rest of their lives to work out the details. He needed time to just be with her. That El Camino could wait another day. Anna's lips grazed his neck.

Or five.

"Are you ordering me to sleep with him?" Shelby Landry asked her smug boss as she stared across the conference room table at him. She loved her job as an FBI agent. It was a lot less messy than working in the garage back home. But in the three years she'd worked for the bureau, she'd never gone undercover alone. And even when she did work on assignment, she'd *never* been told she had to have sex with a man she didn't know. What kind of woman did he think she was?

"I'm not saying that," Rick, Mr. Smug himself, hedged. "As you know, Mason Showalter is the newest partner and latest target at the brokerage firm that has been under SEC investigation, which as of today, we are putting all our resources behind. The SEC has been cracking down on Ponzi Schemes ever since the Madoff embarrassment. The enforcement division has been investigating Feldstein and Baxter Investments for two years and recently asked for FBI support. We agreed to play nice and help out with this inter-agency task, but we need to kick it up a notch."

"So because their investigation has identified Showalter

as a Dom at the highly exclusive club scene, you want her to go undercover as a sexual submissive? I might lead a pretty vanilla sex life, boss, but even I can guess what happens at a *sex* club," Darrell said as he leaned back in his chair and folded his arms. Shelby could always count on Darrell to have her back. He'd mentored her from day one since joining the bureau.

Rick took a sip of the thick, black coffee he always drank and placed the Styrofoam cup next to his notepad. "Her objective is to gain his trust and see what intel she can garner. We don't know if he's privy to the illegal behavior at his firm. If he is, we can't tap his house or office without enough evidence against him. If he isn't, then maybe he can be an asset to us by getting information from the inside."

"Because someone going in to get info has already worked so well," Carson said, referencing Anna's last role as part of their team.

Without acknowledging Carson's comment, Rick turned toward Shelby. "You're not to go in and arrest him or even make a determination of guilt. Just get enough on him so we can get a warrant. The SEC will do the rest. This is still their operation. We'll do our part to make the directors happy and then get out. We have other stuff we should be working on."

"Bet you're glad you are a blonde, eh Viola?" Carson muttered. Carson Childers and Viola Lane rounded out the FBI investigative team Shelby worked on. Lucky for her, the enforcement division hadn't only discovered Mason's need for sexual domination, but also that he had a penchant for brunettes.

With long, flowing locks of the stuff, it was easy for Shelby to understand why she'd been chosen for this task. She'd been singled out for this particular assignment from the beginning. And not because of her mental assets. Hell, her specialty was linguistics. Under normal circumstances, she wouldn't have been considered unless the investment firm under the microscope had documents in Mandarin Chinese the F.B.I. needed her to translate.

"Yeah, that, and I'm married. My husband was all kinds of pissed when I participated in that massage parlor sting op. How would I explain to him that I have to get nasty with a suspect?" Viola shivered.

God, Shelby didn't know if she could do this. She wasn't a virgin, but she was the type of person who had no qualms with the basic missionary position. What had Darrell called his sex life? Vanilla? Yes, she was a big ol' bowl of vanilla. Not even with sprinkles.

Rick sighed. "Let's keep this professional, Lane."

"There's a word for a sex professional, Rick," Shelby finally said. "And prostitutes make a hell of a lot more money than me."

"I know this will be uncomfortable for you, but you don't *have* to have sex with Showalter. Would it make things easier? Maybe. But he and some of the other Doms help with sexual awakening when a woman thinks she might be a submissive. They have been known to engage in activities that do not involve intercourse. This is the angle we are playing."

"That's a big gray area," Darrell said as he glared at Rick.

"I know. But this is our best shot. She can't go in one evening with a wire and hope to get what we need. The man is very private, and it will take time to find out what he knows. If he knows anything, and that's a seriously big *if*."

"So she wears a wire, has some meetings with the man, and we analyze everything first before she gets too involved," Viola said, shrugging. "No need to go in guns blazing yet."

"Won't work," Carson said, frowning. "What if he wants to see her naked? We don't know how he decides to work with a submissive. It's the same reason why she can't wear a wire at all. At anytime she could be asked to strip. We have some very high-tech, inconspicuous devices, but they're not foolproof. Hell, for all we know, he could have some top-notch security measures in place to scramble the frequency, and that's if she doesn't get caught with one on her. The only way I see this working is going in undercover. She'd have to be the eyes and ears for us."

"Agreed," Rick said. "We need Shelby to gain his trust so he'll let her get close to him and maybe even the more personal areas of his life. We only need enough to decide to bring him in to help us out or if we have to play hardball with him."

But the phrase *personal areas of his life* lingered in her mind. "How personal are we talking here?" she asked, gaping at her boss. Sure Carson had just teased about sex, but as the conversation went on, she got the sinking feeling her boss expected more from her than just showing up at the club.

He shrugged. "If you could get a date out of him, get him to take you someplace public, away from the club and any security measures it possesses, that would be a good start. We can record any conversation he has with you without needing a warrant. If you're someplace public, you could be wired without the fear of getting caught. That's just an idea, an option we'd have if it comes to that." He took another sip of his coffee. "The closer you get to him, the better our chances are of getting intel directly from the source."

"So I can't just come right out and ask him if he's involved or if he wants to help," she said with an edge of sarcasm, though it'd be a heck of a lot easier on her if she could do just that.

Rick slammed his fist on the conference table, startling her. "Use your head. That's what someone undercover does, Landry! You play along and get what you need through any means necessary." She'd thought of Anna and the hell the last assignment put her through, lying to the man she loved in the name of justice.

How many lives would this case try to ruin?

She didn't know the answer to that, but Rick had finally answered her question.

Shelby was going undercover in a sex club and would have to sleep with a man who had connections with the company they were investigating. She could fight this assignment and be relegated to a desk job for the indefinite future. Or be transferred out of state like they'd done to Anna.

Or she could suck it up and do what she needed to see an end to this case. There was really only one answer, assuming she honestly had a choice. Prostitution was supposed to be illegal, but apparently not if one's pimp was the federal government.

"Fine. I'll do it."

———

WANT MORE? Be sure to preorder *Shelby*!

———

HEY, y'all!

Thank you for reading my book. :) If you enjoyed it, I'd be very grateful for a review. If you didn't like it, then share that, too... as long as your review is honest, that's all that matters.

And ice cream. Ice cream matters, too.

Want the latest scoop? Be sure to sign up for my Newsletter! I mean, it's not as yummy as ice cream, but nothing ever is.

XOXO,
Mandy

ABOUT THE AUTHOR

Mandy Harbin is a *USA Today* Bestselling author who loves creating stories that explore the complexities of everyday relationships...with some kissing thrown in. She is a Superstar Award recipient, Reader's Crown and Passionate Plume finalist, and has achieved Night Owl Reviews Top Pick distinction many times. She also writes young adult romance as M.W. Muse because teens like kissing, too.

After graduating college and working many years in technology, she threw caution to the wind and began studying writing at the UALR. Years of trashed manuscripts and rejections eventually led to contracts and representation. With over thirty books published, she now serves on the board of her local writing chapter.

Mandy lives in a small, Arkansas town with her husband and their bossy dog, enjoying her own happily ever after...with some kissing thrown in.

mandyharbin.com/newsletter
facebook.com/Author.MandyHarbin
instagram.com/mandy_harbin
bookbub.com/authors/mandy-harbin